# THE BOOK OF
# GRACE

## S.J. CUNNINGHAM

THE BOOK OF GRACE

by S. J. Cunningham

© Copyright 2021 S. J. Cunningham
Paperback Edition

ISBN 978-1-7368136-0-7

*To Rachel, Noah, and Adam. Here's to surviving childhood. I'm so proud of all that you've become, and I thank God every day for the gift of being your mother.*

# CHAPTER ONE

"You cannot leave me here! You cannot leave!" Grace Meyer screamed at her mother as the silver BMW violently backed out of the rutted, rocky drive.

Grace stared at the cloud of dust left behind in where the SUV's tires had spun furiously. Her face was hot with anger, and her throat was swollen with tears. She dug her fingernails into her palms.

She would not cry.

She waited, convinced that her mother would come back for her. There was no way, no matter what Grace had done to invite her wrath, that her mother would leave her only daughter in the middle of the woods. Not that Mariah Barrett was overprotective, but she definitely had her opinions about what Grace should and should not do in her life. Fending for herself in the forest would not have been on her list of goals for her daughter. Her mother had much loftier goals for Grace.

Grace looked around her, kept her breath calm and even.

*Okay,* she thought to herself. *You can deal with this.* After all, hadn't she dealt with much worse?

She looked down at her phone, her only possession, which stared up at her blankly, useless. She doubted there would have been service in the middle of this place, but at least she could have used the compass, she supposed. As it stood, no one—not her friends, not her father, not even her mother's arrogant and dismissive boyfriend—would have any idea where she was.

Grace barely remembered the ride, as if they'd driven through a fog to get here. Wherever *here* was. Her mother had alternated between crying, yelling, and muttering incoherently to herself. Grace had tried to interject a few times, but either her mother hadn't heard her or had chosen to completely ignore her.

Fighting down panic, Grace tried to calm her thoughts enough to pay attention to her surroundings.

The sunshine was soft in the mid-afternoon stillness, and it shone through the large trees around the property. She heard water rushing from a source closeby. The grass was a deep green, and the ground next to the rutted driveway was soft and loamy. The air was totally still.

A long and overgrown driveway behind her ended at a small wooden house in need of a great deal of upkeep. The structure was almost hidden by the bent limbs of the trees and overgrown shrubbery. It was dark and quiet and looked empty but not foreboding.

It looked sad, Grace thought.

She took a long look down the length of the driveway, then turned the other direction toward the road. Whatever was in that house was not for her.

It wasn't a road as much as it was an overgrown path. At one time, Grace thought it might have been a passageway for cars, but foliage, bent from her mother's car tires, covered the pathway, where no trees grew. She started walking down the pathway. The soft undergrowth tickled her bare legs. In the heat of early summer, she wore only shorts and a light t-shirt. There had been no packing and no luggage.

She saw some squirrels and plenty of birds, but no other signs of life presented themselves. No houses, no people out for an afternoon hike. Not that she necessarily wanted to meet another human out here in the lonely afternoon.

On she walked until her shirt stuck to her body and her hair hung damp and limp against her neck.

Finally, she stopped. Listened. The only sounds were water and the happening of the wilderness.

There was nowhere for her to go. And even if she did make it back to a main road, what then? She knew better than to get into a car with a stranger. She supposed she could call someone. Her dad, maybe. But he was too far away.

A slight tickle at the back of her mind. Her father...crying? Could that have been right? She struggled to remember, but even that memory was slipping away…

She didn't spend much time trying to capture the fading illusion. She looked down at her phone and fought the urge to throw it against a tree.

Lifting her long blond hair off her back, she turned around and went back the way from which she had come. Back to the long driveway, ending with the lonesome house.

She regarded the sad structure, and it regarded her back with sagging windows for eyes and a bowed front porch that looked like a yawning mouth. She took a breath and moved forward.

The stairs leading up to the front porch creaked as Grace stepped carefully, and one of the boards lifted slightly as her weight came down. The porch floor itself felt solid enough. The screen door hung off of one of its hinges, and the main door beyond was shut tight. A dilapidated rocking chair sat in the corner of the porch, the seat bottomed out and one of its arms hanging off the side. It moved almost imperceptibly. Grace shivered in the heat. She didn't think the air had enough movement to rock that chair.

She opened the screen carefully, was about to try the door, and then decided that she should knock first. Just in case. She gave three quick raps on the door beyond.

A gaping silence, broken only by distant birdsong,

met her. Grace tried the door. It didn't give.

She knocked again, her heart sinking. Some deep part of her had hoped that there might be the hope of a friendly soul to welcome her, but now she saw the delusion in that.

Slow-burning anger with her mother caused the heat to rise to her cheeks. The anger spread to her father. And then to her friends.

The flash of memory came lighting back. This time the image was of Brandon. Brandon, her boyfriend, her beloved. A twist in her gut and a knife in her heart. Brandon... She tried harder to think back this time. *What had happened, what had happened?*

She laid her hot palm on the smooth, cool door handle and turned. It did not budge. She pushed gently and then more forcefully, but the wood was remarkably solid for an old and dilapidated house. She thrust her shoulder against it, but her one hundred and five pounds didn't carry much power.

She let the crooked screen door shut and glanced back at the sunlight that had begun to dip low and turn golden. There was still daylight left, but not much. If one happened to be lost, what was the chance of reaching a destination that didn't exist before the darkness descended?

Grace leaned her forehead against the cool metal of the screen door. Without her permission, her tears began to flow.

Then, with a loud whoosh, the inside door sucked opened.

Grace jumped and stared at a figure, hidden in the shadows reaching forward from within the house. She scrabbled backward as the figure pushed the screen door open.

The figure slowly emerged from the shadowy interior. Grace's eyes widened, and she felt her bladder spasm.

When the figure emerged fully into the light, Grace found not the scary creature she had feared but a very solid and very real woman.

"Grace," the woman said with a warm smile that lit her entire being. "I thought that might be you."

Grace stared at the woman. "Who are you?" she managed to speak, her voice barely more than a whisper.

"Your mother didn't tell you." It was more of a statement than a question, and Grace shook her head in response.

The woman held the door open, motioning her inside. "It doesn't matter. You're here now, and I'm here now."

The woman didn't say anything further, just waited.

Grace looked over her shoulder, unsure of what to do. Her mother knew this woman? Is that why she had left her here? And yet, she hadn't spoken a word to

Grace on the way here.

"I'm your aunt," the woman said softly. "Mariah's sister."

There was a slight resemblance to her mother. In the eyes, which were softer, and the mouth, which was turned slightly up where her mother's moth was frequently set in a hard, straight line.

"Lucy?" Grace said quietly.

"She told you about me." The statement was filled with a quiet surprise.

"I mean, sort of. Once. I found a picture." She'd been about ten years old and had come into the room, looking for her mother. She'd spotted the worn and grainy photo on her mother's nightstand. Grace hadn't meant to snoop. When her mother discovered her studying the photo, she'd been more dismayed than angry and rather dismissive of the experience. She had told Grace about Lucy but said there wasn't any reason to discuss it because Grace would never meet Lucy. Grace hadn't asked again.

And now, here was the woman, much older, from the photograph.

Lucy said, "We parted ways a long time ago. But your mom holds onto things."

If her mother could completely ignore the fact that her sister existed, Grace wondered how long her mother would hold on to her anger toward her daughter.

"Come in and tell me all about yourself." Lucy held the door wide. "We have a lot of catching up to do."

Grace hesitated. She didn't know this woman. Had no idea if she was who she said she was. But because Grace was out of options, she followed the woman in slowly, and her eyes had to adjust to the dim light in the small place.

Even though the sun was still bright, the trees provided enough shade to keep the inside of the house cool and dark. To her left was a small, neat living room with a comfortable looking sofa, a sitting chair, and two wooden end tables. Books lined shelves on the far wall, and more were neatly stacked on both of the end tables. The interior of the house did not match the ramshackle exterior. This place was homey and comfortable.

To her right was a small staircase that led to a second floor. "Your room will be up there," Lucy said.

"I can't stay here," Grace said. "I have to get home."

Lucy nodded. "You will. But you're here now. And should you decide to stay, we need to make sure you have everything you need."

Lucy kept walking down a short hallway to the back of the house, and Grace followed her into a bright and cheery kitchen. A window over the sink on the back wall looked over the backyard and a large garden.

Grace scanned the garden quietly for a minute. "How long do you think she'll be gone?" she asked.

"Just give her some time. People often need time when they're angry with themselves."

"She's angry with *me*." Mariah was often angry and frustrated with Grace. But this time, Grace couldn't think of what her mother was angry about. Her memory was a fog. She knew she'd done something awful, but she couldn't quite grasp what it was.

"What have you planted in the garden?" Grace asked because she'd rather talk about anything else right now.

"Tomatoes, carrots, peppers, lettuce, some herbs." Lucy pointed to the right. "We also have some chickens who live out there."

At their mention, two fat hens came waddling out of a coop surrounded by wire. "That's Ms. Daphne and Ms. Thelma," Lucy said. "Fred is over there, too."

Grace smiled. "Scooby Doo."

"It was my favorite cartoon, once upon a time."

It was Grace's mother's, too, but Grace didn't say that out loud.

"I'll take you upstairs, and you can freshen up." Lucy smiled. "Let's get you settled, and then we can talk."

Grace followed her aunt up the narrow stairs to a back bedroom with a sloped roof. "Your room is back here. The bathroom is right in between. We'll have to share."

"I didn't pack anything," Grace said, again trying to

remember the events that had brought her here.

"You don't need much here." Lucy smiled at her and smoothed the thin cotton blanket on the twin bed in the small space. She looked as though she wanted to say something else, then thought better of it. Lucy gave Grace's arm a squeeze that was probably meant to be reassuring, then she left the room, shutting the door softly behind her.

Grace sat down on the bed and ran her hand over the thin cotton comforter. It had tiny red flowers on it, like something she would have had when she was a child. The rest of the room was sparse. A small white dresser and a mismatched wicker nightstand were the only other furniture pieces in the room. She walked over to the closet and opened the door. It was small, shallow, and empty. Probably good that she had nothing with her, except her useless phone.

She stood up and walked to the bathroom, also tiny but clean and old, just like everything else in this place. She ran some water that came out in a weak stream and splashed her face; then she looked at herself in the warped mirror. Her face was bare, and her hair fell in natural blonde waves around her face. She didn't look a day of her seventeen years at that moment. She looked about twelve.

Grace turned away from her reflection as the panic rose into her throat again. What was she *doing* here?

She heard a creaking on the floorboards behind

her, and she turned to find Lucy behind her, a towel in her outstretched arms.

Grace lurched away, but instead of appearing offended, Lucy just gave her a kind look filled with patience and acceptance. Even if Grace had wanted to be defensive or terrified, she was just too damn tired.

"I don't know what to do," Grace said, defeated.

"There's nothing for you to do at all right now. Just be with your thoughts."

When Grace didn't answer after a moment, Lucy said, "Come with me."

With a glance back at the small room, Grace followed Lucy down the narrow staircase and into the kitchen.

Lucy had laid out two leafy salads with fresh tomatoes and cucumbers in a light vinegar dressing. There were fresh berries in a bowl in the middle of the table and two tall glasses of water.

Grace couldn't remember the last time she'd actually had a meal. Had actually sat at a table and ate.

"Is this okay?" Lucy asked.

Grace nodded and sat down.

They chewed in silence for a few minutes, and though the food tasted fine—fresh and earthy—she was surprised at her lack of appetite. She could hear the chickens clucking outside, but other than that, there was total silence.

There was something struggling to reveal itself

from the silence. A tumbling, dark and terrifying. Out of control. No screaming, but a swift jolt, a blinding light, and a realization of loss.

Her fork clattered onto the plate.

"Grace," Lucy said, her brow furrowed.

Grace stared up at her. She hated this feeling of isolation and confusion. This was all extremely convenient—her mother dropping her off here along with a long lost relative. But why was she being kept in the dark? Why would no one tell her what was happening? She'd had enough of doing what everyone else told her to do with blind acceptance. She realized that they still thought she was still just a kid, but none of this was fair. Or right. She wanted to know what was going on. "If you're who you say you are, then tell me why I'm here."

Lucy placed her fork on the table carefully and took her time before answering. "You had an accident. And you're having trouble dealing with what happened. Mariah is, too. And that is why you are here."

An accident. Grace tried to make sense of the shards of memory, which didn't seem like memories at all. They were a patchwork of light and shadow, nothing out of any kind of reality.

She thought about her mother, the overachiever. Always pushing, pushing, pushing. Normally, Grace allowed herself to be pushed, but something told her that she'd pushed back this time. "I think she hates me," Grace mumbled. Would her mother abandon her for failing to live up to impossible expectations? The truth was, Grace didn't know, because she didn't know her mother well at all. By mutual agreement.

Lucy said, "She's hating herself right now, not you."

"It was all my fault," Grace said quietly.

Lucy leaned forward. Her green eyes, webbed with soft lines, were kind. "Blame has nothing to do with it. Not now. Do you understand me?"

This woman was completely different than her mother, who was all hard angles and edges. Mariah was beautiful, like sharp, shiny glass. All of Lucy's edges were softened and blurred.

Grace didn't answer, but tears began to well in her eyes.

Lucy sat back and her voice was quiet. "It takes time."

"I don't have time."

"Of course you do. All you have is time. Your summer break is starting."

Summer break was starting? Grace tried to remember, tried to bring back the last vestiges of her school year and her friends. She tried to remember Brandon, but he was an abstract concept, attached to no emotion. He was a two-dimensional picture in a children's book, without context.

She stared down at her plate of half-nibbled salad.

Even though Grace had barely eaten anything, Lucy

cleared the dishes a few minutes later without comment. The sunlight had begun to fade, and the light
outside softened through the trees.

Out of things to say, Grace wandered into the living room and stared at the books on the shelves.

"You can read anything you'd like," Lucy called
from the other room.

Grace ran her hand over the volumes. She had
never liked to read, and it drove her father crazy.
Before he'd gone to law school, he'd been an English
Literature major, and he was always trying to get her to
share his love of books.

Grace stopped at *Tender is the Night*, his favorite
novel. She slid it out and looked at the trees and water
on the front cover. She remembered the beat-up and
earmarked copy sitting on the end table in their old
house when her parents had still been married. Before
the relationship had soured into something that
couldn't be sweetened again.

Lucy came into the room with a dishtowel in her
hands. "Ah, that's a good one," she said, nodding at the
book in her hands. She went over to the shelf and
pulled out a volume.

"*A Wrinkle in Time*," Grace said.

"Have you read it?"

"I don't read." That was a lie. She used to read all
the time. Even if she hadn't wanted to, and she *had*, in
fact, read that particular children's book. It had been a

long time ago, but she remembered it well—the journey between universes, searching for meaning in the battle between evil and divinity.

Lucy nodded to the shelves. "Might be a good time to start."

Grace threw the copy of *Tender is the Night* onto the sofa. "I'm hoping I won't be here that long."

Lucy picked up the discarded book and slid both volumes back into their place as Grace stared at her back.

"Tell me something," Grace said, still determined to get to the bottom of her sudden residence in the middle of the woods. As nice as Lucy seemed to be, why should Grace believe a word that she was saying? "What is her middle name?"

Lucy didn't turn around. "Henriette, for your grandfather."

Grace paused at the correct answer. She's always thought it an odd name. She wasn't sure that her mother had ever told her where the name had come from.

Grace tried again. "Where did she meet my father?"

"Law school. She called him Poindexter at first because of his glasses, and he pretended that he hated her for it, but he was secretly amazed that a woman like your mom would pay attention to him at all."

Grace paused again, at both the correct answer and the new bit of information. Her mother and father were opposites, proving that maybe opposites did attract, but eventually, they repelled. Or one repelled, and the other hung on for dear life. Something like that. To Lucy, Grace said, "My father never mentioned you at all."

"Mariah didn't like to talk about me, and she hated it when he brought up the subject."

"Why?" Grace was now deeply suspicious. It wasn't farfetched that her mother would have disowned her own sister. But Lucy did not seem like competition for her mother. Frankly, she seemed more like someone Mariah would dismiss than hate.

Lucy's shoulders rose and fell with the breath she took. "Because I'd hurt her, and she couldn't forgive me."

"What makes you think she can forgive *me* if you couldn't forgive *you*?"

"That's what we're here to find out."

"I thought I was here because she needed time."

"Yes, Grace, she does. And so do you. Because you have to stop hating yourself."

"Why should I?"

"Because what happened to you and Brandon was not your fault."

Grace squinted her eyes. Brandon. He was there again, floating in her mind, but still detached. "What happened to him?" Grace asked, not wanting to hear the answer but needing to know.

Lucy took a step forward. "This is a lot for you in one day. Why don't you try to get some rest?"

There had been some kind of accident, Grace thought suddenly. She didn't know how she knew that, but she did. She didn't want to think about it. She didn't want to think about *anything*. Because there was a part of her, way down deep, that knew everything had been her fault.

# CHAPTER TWO

G race slept as if she'd never wake up. There were no dreams, just a deep, dark blackness that enveloped her to the point that she became the darkness. But it was a velvet dark, something that blanketed her softly like the softest of kitten fur. She woke only when a shaft of easy light started to make its way through the window. Her awakening was easy and soft, and though she had slept the slumber of the dead just moments before, the light was gentle. She opened her eyes and sighed. Something in her felt free.

She lay there, still and deep for a while, thinking of everything that had happened the day before. She thought of her mother, distraught and sobbing, and her own fear. It didn't rise as swiftly in her throat, but it was still there. How long would she be here? When could she go back to her own life with her friends? She thought of Brandon but stopped short of exploring that further. The freedom that she had felt upon waking threatened to turn to despair, and she closed her eyes, wishing she could go back into the soft darkness.

She couldn't tell how long she had laid there before

she became impatient and swung her legs over the side of the bed. Birdsong sounded outside the window, and from somewhere, again, she heard water rushing.

She caught sight of the fresh pair of shorts and t-shirt on a chair in the corner of the room. They were not hers, but they were the right size, and she put them on.

Though she knew it was pointless, she picked up the cell phone again. It had been everything to her just a few days ago.

A few days ago.

She had a faint memory of picking up the phone and laughing at something on the screen. A dim reminder of her familiar bedroom and a life that seemed ages ago. She felt the same emotional detachment that she'd felt yesterday. That detachment scared her more than anything.

Grace tried to force more memories to come to her. There was something there, just beyond the edge of her mind, but it kept slipping out of her grasp.

She finally gave up, sighed, and went into the tiny bathroom. She had not looked around the previous evening, and she did so now. There was a small shower in the corner. An old toilet and sink appeared to have been installed in the last century. The mirror above the sink was chipped and warped, but Grace looked in it anyway.

Her eyes were puffy and red, and her long hair was

a tangled mess. She opened the cabinet and found a brush caked with old hair product flakes and an elastic band. She managed to pull her hair into some semblance of order. Without a toothbrush, she spread a small amount of gel paste onto her finger and did her best to clean her teeth. Again, she splashed tepid water onto her face. It hadn't appeared yesterday that there were any neighbors close by, and even if there had been, Grace didn't want to see anyone.

She used the toilet, which miraculously flushed and filled up with yellowish water, then she went down the stairs. Other than the faint sound of water and the rustle of the breeze through the leaves, she heard nothing. The living room was empty, as was the kitchen, but there was a plate of buttered bread and a glass of water next to it. She ate and drank quickly, then headed out the back door to the garden she'd seen yesterday.

Her feet were bare, and the grass was soft and wet. She couldn't remember the last time she'd walked in the grass without shoes on. She wriggled her toes. That's when she heard the clucking of the chicken. It looked like dried corn had been thrown there for them to eat. And she watched the fowl pecking around in the grass. The rooster let out a signature call, startling her. She laughed.

These animals seemed completely content, fat and happy, and Grace envied them their simplicity.

She wasn't sure how long she'd stood in the grass. The trees distorted her sense of the sun, both its position in the sky and its heat.

A movement just beyond the small patch of cleared lawn caught her eyes, and she caught sight of Lucy said walking toward her through the brush, carrying two large jugs full of water.

"Where were you?" Grace asked, moving toward her to take one of the jugs.

"There is a spring not far from here," Lucy said, handing her the vessel. "The water is better drinking than well water here."

Grace remembered the yellowed toilet. "Do we need more?" she asked.

Lucy shook her head and set the jug down on one of the faded stairs leading up to the house. Grace did the same. "This will be enough for the day. But later, I'll show you the spring so that you can collect it when we need it."

"What is the water sound?" Grace asked. "Is that the spring?"

"The river."

*The river*, she thought. She knew that somehow, in the back recesses of her memory. She'd heard the sound of the rushing water yesterday but hadn't gone so far as to consider the source. Still, it was not a surprise to her that there was a river nearby. Her subconscious mind seemed to know it.

"I keep forgetting how long it's been since you've been here." Lucy motioned for Grace to follow.

They walked around the side of the house to the front and down the old driveway where her mother had pulled away abruptly the day before. They crossed the overgrown path that was the road and walked through a thicker part of the forest until they found themselves on the bank of a swift snake of water nearly 100 feet across. Rapids danced directly in front of where they were standing.

"It's not this shallow the entire length," Lucy said. "If you drift downriver a few hundred yards," she pointed to a bend in the river, "you can catch some decent trout." Grace followed the direction of her hand and noted the deep mossy green of the river where the rapids had subsided.

"How long have you lived here?" Grace asked. She lifted her face to the warm sun that was now unhindered by the leaves.

"All my life."

Grace looked at her. "And my mother lived here?" That surprised Grace. She couldn't imagine Mariah living in a place that was this quietly untamed.

"When she was a girl, yes. But it isn't a place that Mariah would want to remember."

"Why?"

"For a lot of reasons. Look around."

Grace did.

"We're in the middle of nowhere. Mariah wanted to go somewhere, and she wanted to be some*one*. And if you think the past can hold you back, you do what you can to forget about it."

Her mother was the District Attorney of Franklin County. When she'd been young, Grace hadn't realized what that meant beyond the fact that her mother was gone a lot, and when she was home, she was in her office or reading stacks of documents or hunched over her laptop. As Grace got older, she realized that her mother was kind of a big deal. And while she felt a sense of deep pride about that, she also resented the time it took away from her. But she couldn't quite see the connection to her mother now, and this place.

"She's gotten everything she always wanted, right?" Lucy asked, pulling her back into the present moment.

Grace looked at her sharply, sensing some sarcasm, but Lucy was leaning her head back with her eyes closed. "Can you feel that?" Lucy asked, without waiting for Grace to answer her previous question.

Grace allowed herself to be led from the topic of her mother because she didn't want to talk about Mariah at that particular moment.

"What?" Grace asked.

"The light."

"You mean the sun?"

Lucy hadn't opened her eyes and looked as if she were in a state of ecstasy. "It's perfect today." She went perfectly still, and Grace stared at her. Her long hair hung down her back, and her face was smooth and soft. She looked like a child and a mother and an old woman all at once. "Try it," Lucy said. "Try becoming the sun."

"I don't know what that means," Grace answered, awkward without quite knowing why. Watching Lucy so deeply enthralled with nature seemed invasive somehow. As if Grace was a witness to something private and intimate.

Lucy did not appear to share Grace's discomfort. She opened her eyes and looked over at Grace, then lifted her arms out and up. "Like this." She lifted her face to the sun again, and Grace watched as her whole body seemed to rise, and she began to sparkle.

"How are you doing that?" Grace asked, transfixed. But Lucy didn't answer.

Grace looked around, but there was no one out here. Even though she felt ridiculous, there was nothing stopping her. Grace faced the water and held her arms above her head. She closed her eyes and felt the warmth of the sun on her face and arms. The more she focused, the more she noticed the warmth spreading through the rest of her until the sun's heat permeated her entire being, dissolving all thoughts. Of her mother and father. Of Brandon and her friends. Of what she was doing here. She breathed in the loamy scent of the river, the clean fragrance of the trees, and the warm smell of the sun. She was here. She was everywhere. She was timeless and infinite, but she was small and concentrated. She was everything and nothing, and then she felt herself falling, falling, falling, the sound of rushing water roaring in her ears.

✝ ✝ ✝

The sudden silence was deafening. Grace's eyes snapped open with a gasp, and she stared up at a white plaster ceiling. Light streamed in from the window, illuminating a thin cobweb that had attached itself to the light fixture directly above her. It swayed in the air, appearing and disappearing from her view.

Disoriented, she sat up and looked around. Her fluffy pink robe had been haphazardly discarded on the blue and yellow painted chair in the corner. A pair of pink shorts lay on the floor beside her. The dresser top was cluttered with jewelry and makeup. Her phone vibrated on the nightstand next to her, and she stared at it without immediately picking it up. This was definitely her bedroom—her space—but it felt slightly foreign to her. As if she'd just arrived home after a long trip.

Snippets of the dream clung to her mind. That odd woman in the old house in the forest. She shivered.

"Grace," her mother said, appearing in the door-way. Her voice was urgent and familiar, yet Grace stared at her as if she were a ghost.

"You're still in bed?" her mother said, clearly annoyed. "You're going to be late."

"For what?" Grace's tongue felt heavy in her mouth.

Mariah stared at her. "What is wrong with you?" She came into the room and laid the backs of her fingers against Grace's forehead. "Your SATs are in one hour."

As quickly as she had appeared, she was gone from the room. "I won't be home until at least ten tonight, so make yourself something to eat." She yelled from some other location on the second floor, "And your father is coming to take you to lunch. Make sure you're here to meet him. I don't want to get more nasty texts from him."

Grace somehow doubted that the nasty notes came from her father and not the other way around. She picked up her phone, which had vibrated at least seven more times. She had a bunch of snaps from friends and acquaintances, and she scrolled through them absently.

Her mind wandered back to the dream that had been so real that she'd expected her phone to be completely dead. She looked at a particularly sweet screenshot from Brandon, who had hearts pasted around his face and head.

A sadness came over her, and her throat closed with the emotion. She stared down at the screen. But there was a snap from him right here. He was perfectly fine. She'd just had a strange and very vivid dream.

Her mother was at her door again, fastening a chain around her slender neck. "Grace, I really don't want to have to tell you again to get moving."

"I had a dream about Lucy," Grace blurted out, surprising herself. She hadn't intended to share her thoughts with her mother.

Mariah stared at her, then the necklace slipped from her fingers and fell with a swishing sound onto the hardwood floor of the bedroom. She hesitated for just a second before she bent to pick it up.

"She has chickens," Grace said, the detail of the vivid dream that first came to mind.

"What on earth are you talking about?" Mariah attempted to fasten the chain around her neck but couldn't seem to make her fingers work, and then just gave up.

"There was a river."

"Really, Grace, you're starting to scare me." Grace had the feeling that her mother was trying to make her voice lighter than she felt. Mariah continued, "You know that I'm on this big case. And then I have the Mayor's reception this evening." She cleared her throat. "And *you* have things that you need to be thinking about. First and foremost, your test which is now in less than an hour. This is important, Grace. I shouldn't have to remind you of that."

Grace gave up on the dream. "Are you going with Peter?" she asked, purposefully ignoring the latter part of her mother's short rant.

"Yes, I am going with Peter." Her mother sighed and walked away again.

Grace rolled her eyes. It wasn't that she hated Peter, a senior vice president of something or other at a healthcare company in the city. In actuality, she felt nothing at all for the man, who was smooth and polished and handsome. His hair was silvery-gray, his skin was bronzed. The man practically shone. He didn't give Grace the time of day. She was sure that he felt as little for her as she did for him. To him, she was Mariah's daughter. And that was it.

At the party, her mother would wear the stunning emerald green cocktail dress that fit her petite frame perfectly, and Peter would wear a tailored tuxedo, and they would be the picture of glamor and class and success. And that was all that mattered to Peter. The appearance.

Grace puckered her lips, raised her eyebrows, and stuck her nose in the air. She snapped a picture from her phone and sent it to Brandon. He'd know what she meant.

The thing was, Grace didn't think that Mariah even *liked* Peter. He didn't seem to make her laugh. She didn't talk about him outside the mention of a party or a dinner. Grace didn't see what the point was.

Mariah reappeared one last time. "You'd better do well on these tests. This is your future we're talking about."

Grace didn't answer.

"You *must* get into a good school," her mother continued, "and you need to start thinking about where that is."

Grace had heard this lecture a thousand times, and no answer would please her mother.

"We had this conversation two days ago. Have you thought about it at all since then?"

Grace lifted one shoulder then braced herself.

"Seriously, Grace," Mariah expelled. "This is your life that we're talking about. This should mean everything to you, and you're completely unconcerned." She lifted a hand and let it fall to her side. "We've talked about you getting into a good pre-law program, and if you aren't even going to help, well, I'm not sure how that's ever going to happen."

Grace was positive that she had never once talked about going into a pre-law program. She was interested in becoming a biologist, not a lawyer.

"Don't tell me I need to get your dad involved."

There was zero danger in her mother involving her dad, and frankly, Grace thought it was a little bit lazy of her mother to continue to employ this empty threat. Mariah only brought up his name when it suited her purpose, and even then, it appeared as her mother was bringing it up as a joke. The majority of Mariah's references to her ex-husband involved snide comments blaming him for abandoning them, but Grace knew better. Her mother was a complete control freak, and her dad hadn't been able to take the constant criticism. Not that he was blameless. He'd abandoned Grace while he ran away from her mother. And he was coming to lunch today.

Scott Meyer lived less than two hours away from Grace, and yet she hadn't seen him since Christmas. He had opened his own small law firm in a small town, where he also acted as the township solicitor and was a member of the local school board. His wife Shannon was a lovely young plump woman who taught high school English and had announced her second pregnancy on Christmas morning, where Grace had spent the holiday while Mariah was in the Grenadines with Peter. Shannon was already the perfect mother to their five-year-old twins Emma and Eliot. Grace slept in Emma's tiny twin bed when she visited, and Eliot stared at her and sucked his thumb. He was very damp all the time. They had all moved on without Grace, and Grace decided that she probably wouldn't return.

"Are you listening to me?" Mariah asked, and Grace looked up as her phone buzzed.

"For God's sake, can you not be away from that thing for one minute?" Mariah walked away, disgusted, and Grace was happy that the phone had saved her from a continuation of the lecture.

The truth was, Grace had no idea where she wanted to go to school. A big part of her wanted to go far, far away, but since she'd never really been anywhere outside of her hometown and to her grandmother's condo in Florida, how was she really to know what her options might be? Her mother talked about Stanford and Harvard and Penn and Princeton, but she may as well have been talking about Russia for all the familiarity Grace had with those places.

She sighed deeply as she pushed herself out of bed and went into the bathroom to get ready for the day. By the time she emerged, her mother was gone.

She dressed quickly and ate a container of yogurt while standing at the counter in the kitchen, then climbed into her Honda Civic that her mother had bought her brand new for her sixteenth birthday.

As she drove, she allowed her mind to wander back to the weird dream. Would her mother really abandon her? Maybe, if Grace made her angry enough. She thought about the soft and radiant Lucy, who had treated Grace like an adult. She knew it was only a dream, but Lucy hadn't once asked Grace where she planned to go to college.

Grace pulled up in front of Jessica's square colonial house a few miles from Grace's townhouse. Jessica didn't live in a mansion or anything, but the home was more than respectable, with a perfectly manicured lawn and neat flowers planted around the perimeter.

Jessica walked out the front door first, her sleek, long dark hair swinging behind her as her hips swayed with her gait. Alyssa followed behind her, bouncing, oblivious. Alyssa was sweet, but she did whatever Jessica told her to do.

"I'm going to bomb this," Alyssa moaned as they got closer to the car. "I'm going to have to take it five times."

Jessica shrugged one thin shoulder and pulled open the passenger side door. "I don't even care. My dad will pay for me to go wherever." Jessica's dad owned some sort of road paving business that apparently had contracts all over the state. Despite the modesty of the house, Grace knew that Jessica's parents were loaded. Jessica had a Corvette, but she drove it too fast, and Grace had stopped riding in it. It worked out because Jessica preferred to be chauffeured.

Jessica was someone everyone wanted to be around. She was beautiful, sure, but she also had something else, some dismissive quality that attracted people to her. People did crazy things just to be dismissed by Jessica. And here Grace was driving her around.

Alyssa appeared between the seats, and Grace, said, "Seatbelt."

Alyssa sighed, sat back, and clicked the belt over her lap.

"My mom will kill me if I don't get at least a 1450 on these things," Grace said, continuing the conversation as she steered back onto the road. She laughed as if it were a joke. "Oh, don't worry," Jessica cooed, looking out the window. "I'm sure you'll be perfect, as always."

Grace glanced over at her, wanted to ask her what she meant, but Alyssa piped up from the backseat, "At least your mom cares about you," she whined. "All my mom cares about is my stupid brother."

Grace made a sympathetic face in the rear-view mirror. Alyssa's brother played football at the state's biggest university, and everyone thought he was good enough to play pro next year. He was a frequent mention on the local news stations and sports radio. Alyssa, whose big-boned body and baby face wasn't as useful to her as it was to her brother, usually came in second.

Grace pulled into a spot a few rows from the entrance, and they tumbled out of the car and walked into the doors to the school. As they came up to the large lecture room where the test was being administered, she felt a pair of strong arms around her. "Hey, sexy," Brandon said in her ear, and she melted. Even though she'd been sending him messages earlier, she was relieved to see him after her dream.

"Ugh," said Jessica, her lip curled. "You guys are gross."

"And you're jealous," Brandon flashed her a smile and winked.

"Right." Jessica sneered. "I've got a lot to be jealous of."

She said it under her breath, and Grace frowned. Jessica was strident, but she was rarely mean. Grace also knew that Brandon was the best-looking kid in the school, and for whatever reason, he had chosen Grace and not Jessica. He was finishing his senior year, had been captain of the school's outstanding football team, played basketball, and wrestled. He was going to Wake Forest on a full soccer scholarship in the fall, and this was the last summer that Grace would have with him.

Brandon had thick wavy black hair and a strong chin. There was also a vulnerability to him that was complemented by what appeared to be a very strong sense of who he was as a person. You could never accuse him of being insecure nor arrogant. He simply knew himself.

Even Mariah loved Brandon. He was exactly the type of boy she thought Grace should date. His dad was the CEO of Qualtranics, a startup robotics company that partnered with both major universities in the city, and his mom did philanthropy work. They held garden parties for special causes monthly. They were well-respected not only in the city but throughout the entire country. Brandon went to Europe twice each year, and this summer, he had plans to take Grace with him.

Jessica had seemed especially chagrined about that.

"What are you even doing here? You need to retake your SATs for some reason?" Alyssa asked.

"Nah," said Brandon. "We came to wait for the pretty ladies. We're going to shoot some hoops in the gym until you're done."

Grace turned around and held Brandon's hand as they walked in together. She was deeply happy right now. No matter how demanding her mother was, no matter how jealous Jessica was, Brandon would always be there for her.

# CHAPTER THREE

"Brandon, Brandon, Brandon," Grace whispered as the sun warmed her face. Something pierced her reality, and she sat up with a start, her heart beating wildly. "Whoa." She sucked in air as she stared at the rapids in front of her. She was aware of Lucy beside her. She stared over at the older woman.

"What happened?" Grace asked, gasping. She struggled to get her bearings about her and looked around. She remembered being here, in this exact spot. She looked up at the sun in the sky. It appeared to be in exactly the same position.

"Did I fall asleep?" Grace asked.

Lucy's eyes were shut, and she radiated peace and patience. "Maybe for a minute."

Grace rubbed her face. "Was I just dreaming?" she asked. "Or remembering…" her voice trailed off. She would have sworn she had just been talking to her mother, riding in that car, actually experiencing Brandon's arms around her.

Lucy didn't respond, and Grace stared into the gurgling rapids, wrapping her arms around her knees.

Finally, Lucy said, "Dreams are just a reflection of the experience," she said. "But sometimes they are more valuable than the experience itself because the dream can give you more information. More insight."

Her mother's insistence on choosing the right school, the test scores, even the need for approval from Jessica and Alyssa had brought with it a palpable anxiety. Sitting here along the river's bank—none of that seemed important. But it was still there, waiting for her.

Lucy stood and brushed off her jeans. Her brown hair fell loosely around her shoulders, and her face was utterly calm and still. Grace could not believe that this was her mother's sister. "How old are you?" Grace asked, aware that the question may be rude. She would have never thought of being that bold with Mariah.

The answer came without hesitation. "Today, I am forty-two."

"You're older than my mother."

"By a year, yes."

"You seem much younger."

Lucy laughed. "She wouldn't like to hear that."

"But it's true. And kind of amazing. She takes good care of herself."

"She takes good care of her skin, and she exercises. She takes care of her body."

Grace cocked her head, looking up at Lucy.

"She doesn't take care of her soul," Lucy explained.

"Oh, we don't go to church. I've gone with my dad a few times, though. All those fake people acting like they're holy." She'd watched a woman smile sweetly at her and her father, then turn around, whisper, and titter with another woman. Grace had known instinctively that they'd been talking about her—the discarded daughter. After the service, there had been a pot-luck dinner in the cavernous church basement, and she'd watched the minister's wife gorge herself on ham and fried chicken and potato salad and talk with her mouth open to the judging woman beside her while the minister himself talked to the same slim and attractive brunette the entire time.

Lucy reached down to help Grace up. "Don't you think, though, that those people are just looking for something to guide them through their hardships?"

"I think they're checking a box."

"Some of them, probably yes," Lucy agreed as they walked from the sun into the shaded forest toward the house. "But some of them are peace seekers."

"What about the ones who gossip and talk about people behind their backs?"

"Your feelings about those people have more to do with you than they do with them," Lucy responded. "And their words about you have more to do with them than they do about you. People experience life through the filter of their own existence."

They reached the house, and Lucy opened the door

for Grace to enter. All of the windows in the house were opened, and a clean and fresh breeze blew between the space around them. Grace breathed in the scent of the forest and the unique smell of the wood in the room. There was calm here.

Lucy continued, "And you've perceived that entire observation through the filter of *your* own experience. What you understood and the intentions of that other person have very little relation to one another."

"That's all great, talking about it now. To think back about it then. But at the time, it was meant to make us feel…less than her, somehow."

"Are you less than her?"

"No."

"Then it doesn't matter what she said at all. The energy of her words and thoughts gets directed back at herself if you give them no power in your own experience."

They walked into the tiny kitchen, and Grace was surprised to find that she felt very at home here. A white cat appeared from nowhere and sleekly wound its way around Lucy's feet as she reached into a cupboard.

"Who is this?" Grace asked, bending over to offer her hand to the new addition.

"This is Logi. He comes, and he goes, but he's always here."

Logi approached Grace's outstretched hand and

rubbed his silky head against Grace's palm. Then she looked over at Lucy and meowed.

Grace laughed. "Is he asking you if I'm okay?"

"No, he's telling me that you are okay."

"You can talk to him?"

"Not with words," Lucy said and smiled. "But all beings have the ability to communicate. Don't you think?"

"I've never really thought about it." Grace had never had an animal. Her mother had said that they hadn't had the time for one, and she'd been right. Her dad and Shannon had a big, sweet, dumb Labrador named Bubba, who danced around Grace and slobbered on her hands when she tried to pet him. Eliot and Emma adored the thing, tried to ride him, fell asleep on his chest and haunches. Grace had always been tentative with him, but he seemed to love her anyway.

Lucy boiled some water on the stove, and Grace sat down at the table. Logi jumped up on the table beside her and stared at her.

As Grace stroked the soft, sleek fur of the cat, she said to Lucy, "I'm not really hungry."

Lucy responded, "Energy."

When Grace cocked her head, Lucy continued, "The food."

That had been something Grace's mother used to say when Grace was younger and full of fire and speed and hadn't wanted to eat. It was something Mariah hadn't said for a while since she was afraid that both she and Grace would gain weight. Grace was far from heavy, but she scoured her body each morning for a new roll on her stomach or any dimples of fat on her butt.

"Was my mother overweight when she was young?" Mariah, having been overweight as a child, would explain her treatment of Grace.

"She was a waifish little thing." There was a rhythmic chopping on the counter. "I was the thick one." Lucy lifted a shoulder, her back still to Grace. "It doesn't matter at all."

"At home, it does."

Lucy looked over her shoulder at Grace. "At seventeen, you shouldn't be worrying unless you have some sort of health issue."

But Grace knew that if you wanted the right boys to like you—the right friends, the right opportunities, it mattered very much. And Brandon was the right boy with the right background, who had brought her the right friends.

Lucy continued, "If people are judging you based on looks and weight, then do you really want to be friends with them at all? Those aren't your people, nor are those your opportunities. You'll only be good enough until someone that they think is 'better' comes along."

"How long has it been since you've lived in the real world? That's the way it works there, you know."

"You don't think this is the real world?" Lucy motioned around her, the knife slicing through the air. She didn't sound angry, but she did sound firm.

"Well, I mean, it's real, but it isn't real, like with other people and situations and things that you have to deal with. You're alone out here. This isn't what reality is normally like."

"Whose reality?"

Grace thought for a minute. "Mine. Or my mother's. Or my father's." Grace shrugged. "This is like hiding."

Lucy stopped what she was doing and turned around. "Hiding from what?"

"Hiding from reality."

"Interesting. Do me a favor." Lucy came closer, lifted her arms above her head, pressed her palms together while shutting her eyes, and lifted her face to the ceiling. "Do this for me."

Grace thought it was weird, like everything else out here in the woods. But she would do it.

"Take a deep breath and fill your lungs."

Grace did as she was told.

"Pay attention to the feeling of one palm against the other for a minute."

Grace thought about her hands and her breath, and the longer she sat there, the more difficult it became to determine where one hand began and the other ended.

"When you sit like this, do you feel any less real than you did the last time you were home?"

Grace opened her eyes and put her hands down. She considered the question. "As a person—as a human being—I feel very real here," she said. "Maybe I'm talking about the experiences."

"Ah, now the experiences are not the same." Lucy went back to cooking, sliding vegetables into the boiling water on the stove. "But no experience is the same, is it? There are different people, different thoughts, different feelings. You're always going to be right in the middle of those unique experiences. But it's important not to think one thing will define the rest of your life. You're weight, your looks. Those physical qualities will change, but it's what is inside that will determine your path forward. How you deal with different realities."

Lucy rummaged in a cupboard next to a sink, pulling out two plates, which she set down in front of them. Then she served the simple boiled vegetables.

After they'd eaten, Lucy took Grace through the trees on a path to the freshwater spring, where they gathered jugs full of water and collected eggs from Daphne, Thelma, Wilma, and Betty, while Fred watched them, clucking the whole time. They talked companionably about Lucy and Mariah when they'd been children. Grace was surprised to find herself laughing at stories about the two sisters sneaking into a cow pasture not too far away through a broken fence, only to find that when they'd returned, the fence had been repaired and was now electrified. Too far from anyone to get help, they'd been mildly electrocuted making their way home. Grace's grandmother had been horrified, especially since there had been a bull amid the herd of cattle. But they had returned un-scathed.

Time seemed to pass at a different pace here, and when they'd finished the chores, it was almost evening.

"Can I ask you a question?" Grace asked.

Lucy lit two lanterns on either side of the fireplace mantle. "Of course. And I'll answer if I can."

"What are you doing out here by yourself?"

"I think what you're asking is, why have I never gotten married or had children?"

Grace wasn't sure if that's what she'd been asking at all, although it was odd that this vibrant woman existed out here alone, with no other discernable connections. "I just mean," Grace said, "it's quiet and lonely."

"Lonely. Now there's a word." Lucy sat down in an armchair in the living room. "I'm not lonely at all. I'm quite content with this existence."

And she did look content. Happier than Grace had ever seen either of her parents.

"But who do you talk to?"

"Logi, the hens, the air, the sky, the water, the wind.

They're all good listeners, and they have plenty to say if you're willing to still yourself long enough to hear it. But I'm comfortable with myself too. And that takes some practice."

Grace couldn't stand being alone. There were way too many thoughts—whole ones, half ones, firm ones, and slippery ones. And she couldn't hold on to any of them at all. Sometimes she thought she must be out of her mind with the noise inside her own brain.

She had curled into a corner of the sofa, and even now, the thoughts were running rampant. What was her mother doing? Where was her father, and why hadn't he at least come for her? Did he even know where she was? What had happened to Brandon? Did it have something to do with why her mother was so angry with her?

"How about you?" Lucy asked.

Grace looked up.

"Are you lonely?"

Grace shrugged. "I have a lot of friends."

"Not the answer to that question, you know."

Grace hesitated and thought about how busy her mother was and her father's preoccupation with his new family. Alyssa and Jessica were probably her closest friends, but Grace didn't think they wanted to hear about her thoughts and fears or anything that didn't focus on them and their lives. At least anything that went below the surface. Even Brandon, who she loved with her whole being, didn't know how messed up she was inside.

She thought about her three friends from her childhood—Ava, Megan, and Kate. They had been close friends for years, but she'd traded them in for newer and shinier friends. She wasn't proud of that, of how she sometimes ignored them in the hallways when she saw them. She had pretended not to see Megan in the grocery store a few weeks before.

"I sometimes feel alone in this life," Grace admitted.

"I used to feel alone, too."

"What did you do about it?"

"Tried to fill myself up with things that ended up making me feel emptier than when I'd started. And the things that might have helped—activities with people I connected with, sports, art—I pushed those away. I put all of my trust in one person, and it wasn't the right thing to do."

"But you're fine now."

"It's a different time, and experience has shaped me into a different person. For a long time, I wasn't okay."

Grace was still. "I'm okay, though," she said in a small voice.

"You're safe."

"Was my mom that way?" Grace couldn't imagine her ambitious, determined, focused mother being any other way.

"Your mom dealt with her loneliness differently than I did, and I suspect differently than you do. She still does. She's spectacularly independent and loathe to admit that anything could penetrate her. When we were young, I wanted to be like that." Lucy's voice was heavy. "I wanted to be her. She was strong, and I was weak. I thought that she knew I wasn't as strong as she was."

"Because you weren't like her?"

"Now, I realize that it wasn't quite that she thought I was weak. I scared her with my willingness to show my emotions. I made myself vulnerable. And in her mind, that's when you can get the most hurt."

Grace understood. "I think she's right."

"It's also when you discover the truth about yourself and other people. If you live in armor for your entire life, you never find out exactly what's real. You never find out exactly what love is. You have to put yourself out there."

"But you never found love."

Lucy laughed. "Because I never got married and had babies? No, I didn't do those things. But I found all the love." Lucy shut her eyes, and her breathing slowed.

Grace watched her for a while. Her aunt looked absolutely at rest and completely at peace. Without the animation in her face, she looked even younger than she did when she was awake. Grace stared at her, trying to find herself and her mother in this unconventional woman who chose to live by herself in the forest. She thought about what Lucy had said, that her mother had thought that Lucy was weak. Grace wondered again why Mariah had chosen to bring Grace here. And when she was coming to take her home.

# CHAPTER FOUR

G race blinked, and she was staring down at her test paper. Her breathing picked up. Her heart pounded in her chest.

She looked up and glanced around the room; at first, surprised and then shocked. The large lecture hall was filled with students hunched over their papers. The only sounds were the scratching of pencils and shuffling of feet, along with the occasional cough or clearing of throats.

What was happening to her? She had no memory of sitting down in this classroom. She had no memory of filling out this test, though looking at the answer sheet, it appeared as though she was almost done.

Were these answers correct? There was no way of knowing now and no time to go back over the answers.

Mr. Anderson, her Psychology teacher, who was also today's proctor, was watching her from the front of the room. He walked toward her and, when he reached her desk, asked, "Everything okay, Miss Meyer?" His tone was neutral. This man neither liked her nor hated her. She was just a student in a class of his.

"I'm not feeling well," Grace whispered.

A few students looked their way.

"You have ten more minutes," he answered. "Can you wait that long?"

Grace looked down at her paper and then up at him. "I think I messed up."

"You'll have plenty of time to retake it if you don't get the scores that you want."

Her head started to swim, and she lifted a hand to her cheek.

"Just finish it up. It'll be okay." He gave her a half-hearted smile and then walked away to take his place at the front of the room.

She read over the first part of the essay that she'd written, not even aware of what the prompt was. How could this have happened? And what was wrong with her? Did she need to go to the hospital?

Mr. Anderson announced that the time was up, and the students all rose at nearly the same time, like a great amoeba made of individual high school students. She watched them moving passively toward the front of the room, and the voices slowly increased in volume. After most students had walked forward, she rose and handed in the useless paper before walking numbly out of the room. Alyssa and Jessica made their way over.

"I failed it." Alyssa's high-pitched and insincere wail grated on Grace's nerves.

"You don't 'fail' it," Jessica corrected. "You just probably got a terrible score." She turned to Grace, her blond hair swooshing in an arc behind her. "How about you, Einstein? 1600?"

Grace regarded Jessica coolly for a minute. The bite in her voice had been unmistakable, and Grace wondered why she was just now noticing how Jessica treated her. Jessica stared back at Grace, who noticed that Jessica's hair was naturally blond, made blonder with expertly placed highlights. Her lips weren't as pouty as Jessica made them look with lip gloss and a particular way of making her mouth into an O and pulling her cheeks slightly together. But her eyes were huge, blue, globe-like. Their wideness gave her the appearance of innocence until you looked a little closer and saw the glint in them. If Grace had to guess, she'd say it was the glint that pushed her from attractive to desirable to guys. But to Grace, the glint made her seem mean and small.

Grace didn't need to answer Jessica's questions because Brandon, Eli, and a kid named Nate were coming toward them, jostling each other as they walked out the door. Jessica lost interest in Grace.

"Look at these losers," Jessica yelled, and a few other students turned to look at her. She ignored them. "You all ready for college?"

"Hell, yes," Nate yelled and gave a loud whoop for good measure.

Mr. Anderson appeared at the door of the lecture room with a scowl on his face.

"Come on, man." Eli held his hands out in the teacher's direction. "It's Saturday. You can't get mad at us on a *Saturday*."

"Go," Mr. Anderson said. Laughing at the hilarity of the situation, the group of students cackled and tripped over themselves, moving to the exterior doors.

Grace hung back. She felt disoriented and had a dull headache behind her eyes. Brandon noticed and lingered with her. "You okay?" he asked.

Grace gazed up at him. She wished she could tell him about the confusing blackout periods, but she didn't think he'd understand. "I don't think I did particularly well," she admitted quietly, instead.

"Aw, it's okay." He pulled her against his side. "You have some time." Brandon was a good guy, she knew. He might hang out with those other Neanderthals, but he wasn't like them deep down. She *knew* that.

There was something else that she couldn't quite put her finger on; some worrisome thought deep in her mind that made her want to hold onto Brandon a little more tightly. "You're right," she said. "It's almost summer. We should be having some fun."

"Now, that's what I like to hear," Alyssa yelled in their direction. Alyssa was sweet most of the time, but she could party a lot. Like Jessica, she had artful highlights but on mousy brown hair. Unlike Jessica, her lips were naturally pouty—almost an old-fashioned bee-stung look. Overall, she was prettier than Jessica, but she had no glint. With Alyssa, what you saw was what you got. And sometimes that wasn't a lot. She tended to be popular with all of the guys, but only for a short period.

Brandon and Grace had caught up with the rest of the group, and they all tumbled outside into the late spring warmth. The weather was unseasonably warm— a precursor to the promise of a fun-filled summer before half of their group headed to college and adulthood. None of them wanted to think about that yet.

At the front of the group, Nate walked backwards and faced them all. "My parents are gone for the weekend. Everyone is invited. Right now."

"Hell, yeah," laughed Brandon. There was a general cry of agreement from the group.

Grace pulled back. "I'm meeting my dad for lunch," she said to Brandon. Before he could respond, Jessica was in front of her.

"Oh, that's such a *shame.*" She smiled sweetly and wasn't nearly as pretty as she'd been just a second earlier.

"I haven't seen him since Christmas," Grace continued, not sure who she was addressing.

Eli hung back to stand next to Jessica. "I wish I hadn't seen my dad since Christmas," he said. Grace, he goaded, "Come on."

"Yeah. Come on, Gracie," Brandon coaxed. "You can see your dad anytime."

"Yeah, come on, Gracie." Jessica smiled at her in her saccharine way. "You can see your dad anytime," she parroted Brandon's words.

Grace's face heated. "I actually can't," she bit back. "He lives two hours away."

Jessica snorted, and sensing conflict, Alyssa appeared, trying to diffuse the situation. "Just come when you're done," she offered, pouting her lips prettily.

Brandon nodded. "Yeah, do that."

"There will be so many ladies there. You'll hardly be missed." Nate elbowed Brandon, who laughed. But Brandon had the decency to look at least a little sheepish when he glanced at Grace.

A wave of nausea churned through Grace. She already resented that her dad was coming here. She also knew that he would be hurt if she blew him off. And if she didn't show up, he'd be worried, and he'd call her mom. Mariah would sniff her out—she had a way of finding out all sorts of private information—the party would be busted, and it would be all her fault.

"Wait," Alyssa said suddenly. "Grace picked us up. How do we get to Nate's?"

Jessica pouted her lips again and sucked in her cheeks. "Oh, poor Lyssa. Don't you see these four gorgeous guys we have to choose from?"

Jessica's long fingers settled around part of Brandon's bicep.

Brandon pulled away quickly and grabbed Grace's hand. "I'll be in touch, okay?"

Grace didn't respond. She had watched Jessica flirt with Brandon before, but she hadn't paid much attention. Today, her comments were more aggressive. And even though Brandon was doing and saying the right things, something about him seemed evasive. Was she imagining it?

The group moved away from her together, a wave of bodies spewing laughter and fun. And she was left by herself beside her car, feeling disconnected and very alone.

She watched them for another minute. None of them turned around to wave.

Other students were also pulling out of the parking lot. She watched Nate's Mustang spin into a burnout on the pavement as it screeched out away. It made an angry black mark on the asphalt, and she knew he'd probably be called down to the office on Monday.

She saw Brandon's car move much more responsibly in the same direction. She tried to make out the shape of any passengers, but he was too far away.

An older model Buick pulled up beside her, and she saw that it was Megan, her old friend with whom she'd spent so much time and shared so many secrets. Before Jessica and Alyssa. Before Brandon. Heat flooded

Grace's face. But standing next to her car, there wasn't any place that she could duck and hide.

"Hi," Megan said a little tentatively through her window.

"Hi," Grace said back, guarded and feeling like a jerk as she usually did when she ran into her former crowd.

"How did the test go?"

"Okay," Grace said, lying. Even then, she recognized that she could tell Megan the truth, and Megan would listen and offer either sound advice or the appropriate sympathy. Grace didn't deserve that from Megan anymore.

"Have you looked at any schools?"

"Not yet," Grace answered. "My mom has big plans for this fall, though. You know how she is."

Megan laughed. "Yeah, your mom is something else."

There was a pause, and Grace said, "How about you?"

"I thought maybe you'd heard. I've been talking to the swim coach at Rollins College. I haven't officially applied or been accepted…" She trailed off and tucked a piece of her short brown hair behind her ear. "I'm looking forward to it."

"I hadn't heard," Grace said. She lifted her hand in Megan's direction. "Congratulations." She meant it, but she felt something else too. It wasn't jealousy.

Maybe wistfulness. There was a time when Megan would have shared this kind of news with Grace first, and they would have celebrated together. In any case, she was happy for her old friend.

"Do you think you'll swim?" Megan asked.

"Oh, god no," Grace said, maybe too quickly. "I'm out of shape," she continued. "And, that's…just not me anymore."

The expression on Megan's face shifted—her eyes hardened, and her mouth turned down. "Well," she said.

They both looked to the side, and then Grace said, "It was nice talking to you."

Megan nodded, her mouth still downturned. "You too. See you around."

"Yeah."

After Megan pulled away, Grace climbed into her car and turned left toward the highway where she was meeting her dad at a popular upscale barbecue place that had decent wings. It had been her choice, and she'd made it not only because the food was good but also because the atmosphere was loud and there would be plenty of distractions. It was also a popular hangout for kids from school. Some of them might be headed there after the test. They may not be her closest friends, but they'd do in a pinch. She had nothing at all in common with her dad.

She pulled into the restaurant lot, parking in a spot

a few rows back from the entrance. When she looked at her phone, she saw a text from her dad. He was seated in a booth by the windows in the back. She sat in her car for a minute before she'd taken enough breaths to fortify herself.

Finally, Grace walked in, and there he was, immediately waving to her from a booth. The restaurant was crowded with families and older couples, but she saw no one from school. She walked toward him, and he stood to hug her as she approached.

The embrace was awkward—he'd tried to hug her fully, and she'd offered only the side of her body. It was just like everything else about their relationship.

"I thought maybe you'd bring Shannon and the kids," she said as they sat down. She hadn't thought that at all, but she knew it would make him feel guilty for the few times he'd arranged to see her without them.

"No, no," he said, pushing his thick black glasses up on the bridge of his long nose, then placing his hands on the table in front of them. "It's just me today. Sorry to disappoint."

Just like him to miss the slight sarcasm in her tone and turn the guilt back around on her. She didn't contradict him.

"How are you?" He managed to speak at the same time as the youngish and world-weary server who approached with water for her and asked if they needed more time.

He held up two fingers. "Just a few minutes."

Looking bored, she nodded and shuffled away.

"I'm okay," she said, picking up where he left off.

"SATs great?"

"Why does everyone assume that?" Her tone was harsh. She shook her head. "Actually, no, they weren't, but don't tell my mother that."

His mouth slackened. "What happened?"

"Maybe I'm not as smart as you both seem to think I am."

His face looked like it actually might crumple. He would have been a handsome man, she thought, if he weren't as apprehensive.

And Grace didn't want to do this. She didn't want to have a hostile conversation with her father today. She just wanted to get through this lunch as quickly as possible. "I'm sorry," she said. "It's fine. They were fine."

He looked at her intently. Then his face broke out into a wide smile. "Oh, Grace. You had me going there for a second."

She forced a halfhearted smile in return. "Yeah."

"So, schools? Thoughts yet?"

She thought about Megan and her muted excitement about...Rollins, was it? Grace wasn't even sure where that was. "Talk to Mom. She'll tell you all about *my* thoughts."

Her dad shrugged. "You know your mom. She has strong opinions. But you need to do what's right for you. If you want to go visit any of them, I'd be happy—"

She held up a hand. "It's okay, Dad, really. I got this."

He opened his mouth, then thought better of it and looked down at his menu. She did the same, and when the server came back, she ordered a chicken Cobb salad and an iced tea. Her dad ordered a buffalo chicken sandwich.

"This is an interesting place," he said, looking around. "Nothing like it in my neck of the woods. Do you and your friends come here?"

"Sometimes." There was a long moment of silence. Grace looked at her phone, but she hadn't heard directly from any of her friends, though there were notifications from her friends' stories.

She opened the Snapchat app and saw Jessica's story. She was floating next to Brandon in the pool. They weren't touching, but her hands turned to ice.

"I don't even know your friends," her father mused, taking a sip of his water.

"You don't live here," she mumbled while desperately searching for any other incriminating pictures.

"No," he agreed. He placed his palms flat on the table and spread his fingers apart. "Grace," he said.

While part of her heard him, she didn't look up from her phone. There were other snaps from people at the party, and she was scouring them for a glimpse of Jessica and Brandon in the background. She was primed and ready to see something upsetting, but the pressure in her chest loosened with each innocent photo.

"Grace," he said again, more firmly.

"What?" she snapped.

He sucked in a breath, and she sat back in the booth. She also took a deep breath and put the phone on the table beside her. "I'm sorry," she said.

He nodded.

She should have gone to Nate's. It was a mistake to let Brandon go without her. She was practically inviting him to cheat on her with Jessica. Jessica, whose tiny waist and concave stomach would be accentuated by the tiniest of swimsuits. Jessica, who bragged about her sexual prowess and had pictures to prove it.

Grace had thought Jessica's stories were funny and a little sad—until now. Now, they seemed threatening. Grace hadn't done much at all, physically, with Brandon. That was a step she wasn't sure she wanted to take yet, even though she knew it made her a complete dork. Maybe she shouldn't have listened to the prudish cautious part of herself and tried to be just a little bit more like her more adventurous friends.

Her dad cleared his throat, bringing her back to the present, and she forced herself to look at him. Except for the lines around his eyes, he looked exactly how she remembered him as a little girl.

His face was serious. "Shannon and I have been talking, and—"

"All right," the server said, appearing beside their table and holding the tray on her shoulder. She was oblivious to any other conversation that may have been taking place. "I have a chicken cobb salad." She placed the order in front of Grace. "And a buffalo chicken sandwich." She set her dad's plate down. "Can I get you anything else? More water? Iced tea?"

He shook his head. "Thank you," he said firmly.

She walked away, and Grace stared at her salad, not in the least bit interested in eating it. She took a bite anyway while her dad pushed his sandwich around on the plate.

"Shannon and I have been talking about the baby, and Emma and Eliot," he said, then incongruously chose that moment to take a bite of his sandwich.

Grace waited and understood why her mother might have been impatient with this man. Mariah was all about efficiency. Scott Meyer took the long way around, always. She wondered how they'd ever gotten together in the first place.

He swallowed and took a drink of water. Then he said, "We were wondering if it was possible… If you might like to come and live with us."

Grace paused her fork halfway to her mouth then set it back down in the bowl.

"For the summer?" she asked. Of course, the answer would be no to that question, along with any other time-frame that he had proposed. But she was shocked that the question had been asked to begin with.

Appearing buoyed by not being immediately rejected, his face became more animated. "To start," he said, "but even longer than that. We'd love to have you there permanently."

She thought about Brandon, and her body revolted. She shook her head quickly, and her dad held up his hand. "You don't have to make a decision today. I'm just asking you to think about it."

She seemed to have a hard time catching her breath. "You talked to Mom about this?"

"Well, not yet. We thought it was best to talk with you first. Get your thoughts. But your mom—well, we know how busy she is, and she's dating that guy. It seems like good timing."

"It will be my senior year." Grace was genuinely shocked by how this conversation was going.

"And wouldn't it be great to have a fresh start? Get you ready for college? Shannon teaches at the high school, and it's actually one of the best schools in the state. If you look at their scores—"

"Dad," Grace interrupted. "All of my friends are here. I've taken all of my classes here. It doesn't make any sense for me to start over now."

"I know it seems like a lot, but I think if you noodle on it for a while, you'll come to like the idea."

"I will stop you right there and tell you that I will not like this idea, no matter how long I *noodle* on it." She had raised her voice, and a few diners close-by glanced in her direction. She didn't care, but she knew that her dad would.

He dropped his chin to his chest and then unenthusiastically took another bite of his sandwich. Grace pushed her salad away.

"Why are you asking me this now?" she asked. "I'll be going to college in a year."

"We thought it would be nice for you to get to know your brother and sister and new sibling before you went to school," he said. "You barely know the twins, and you'd be in this new one's life from the start."

"For a year," she clarified. "Before I go away. A baby wouldn't even remember me." She shook her head. "And I have no interest in making new friends, no matter where it is. It's bad enough that I'll have to leave everyone after next year. I'm not doing that twice."

"I'm just asking you to think about it, Grace."

"And I'm telling you, it's not going to happen."

She watched his face change from passive and disappointed into something much uglier. "I told your mother that she was going to make you selfish. Spoiled and selfish."

"Selfish?" she was incredulous. "Are you kidding me? Number one—I don't see how not wanting to move in with a bunch of strangers the summer before my senior year could possibly make me a selfish person. And number two—you *abandoned* us. You have no right to call anyone else selfish."

"You're just like her," he shot back. "Placing blame when it's lying right at your feet."

Her head snapped back as if she'd been slapped. "You left because of me?" she whispered.

His eyes widened. "No, no. Grace, that's not what I meant."

Grace grabbed her purse from the seat beside her and picked up her phone.

"Grace, please," he rose and stood in front of her. Now everyone in the restaurant was looking at them. She noticed their server staring at them from the front of the dining room. "Please, listen," her father continued.

She wouldn't look at him, but she didn't want to make a scene in the restaurant despite her earlier indifference. She sat down and furiously scrubbed a hot tear from her cheek, willing herself not to cry.

"Your mother," he started and cleared his throat, leaning forward. "I'm going to share some adult information with you, but I think you can handle it. I also think you have a right to know." He paused, and when she didn't respond to that negatively, he continued. "When we divorced, your mother wasn't making very much money as a clerk in the District Attorney's office. I was making much more at the firm downtown where I was working at the time. When the judge set the alimony and child support payments, it was based on the amounts we were making back then. And I was making a lot more than and working many more hours than I do in private practice now. And now I'm supporting a lot more people."

"What does this have to do with me?"

He sighed, spread his hands in front of him. "With the new baby on the way, Shannon would like to quit teaching. But we don't know if we can swing it financially if we lose her income. And I'm kind of stuck in my job at the moment. There are higher-paying jobs in the city, but I can't commute to the city from our place."

"Then move out here," Grace said flatly.

"I can't do that to them."

"But you can do it to me."

"That's not reasonable," he said, gently. "The kids are young, and Shannon's folks are there. But you only have one more year left. If you move in with us, I could go back to the court, and the child support payments would go away."

Grace looked at him. "If you're making less money than mom, why wouldn't you just go back and get the amount reduced?"

He hesitated, swallowed.

She tilted her head and narrowed her eyes. "Because you already have." Her mother hadn't said anything to her, but she was sure she'd overheard a conversation between her mother and one of her friends. "If I come and live with you, she'll have to pay *you*, won't she?" It wasn't really a question. She already knew the answer.

"It isn't that simple," her father said.

"But it *is* that true," Grace said and stood up again. She picked up her phone. "You know, mom may not be perfect, but at least she doesn't use me as currency."

He had the sense not to say anything else.

The little girl at the table behind them let out a wail and knocked a cup of milk onto the floor. "Lucy," the young mother exclaimed. "What are you doing?"

Grace stared at the little girl, who looked back at her with gray-green eyes and a perfectly clear smile on her face.

*Lucy*, she thought to herself. Lucy was the name of the woman in the dreams that were not really dreams. The name of the woman in the hazy alternate existence. The name of the woman who had claimed to be her aunt—her mother's sister.

Grace looked back at her father. "Lucy," she repeated. "You knew her." Although she didn't really want to talk to him right now, he had information that she needed.

He looked up, startled and confused by the change in topic. "Excuse me?"

"She knew your favorite book was 'Tender is the night.' I think that's true."

"Grace, what are you talking about?"

"She's mom's sister."

"Yes, I know who she is, but I didn't know her. Your mom must have told you about the book."

"No, Lucy said she knew you."

He started to get up. "Grace. You're scaring me."

She held up her hand and looked down at the little girl, who had gone back to hitting her spoon against the table. After that momentary connection, the child didn't look at Grace again.

"Lucy is dead," Scott Meyer continued. "She died before I met your mother."

Grace put her hand to her head, and then she felt herself falling.

# CHAPTER FIVE

When Grace opened her eyes, she was in the small bed in the house in the forest. She remembered everything about the lunch with her father. And she didn't think it was a dream at all. She looked out the window, and a light rain was falling. She slid up the pane of glass, and the smell of old wood, earth, and humid air filled her nostrils.

The birds were quiet, but the rush of the rapids sounded in the distance.

What was happening to her?

She walked downstairs and heard voices coming from the kitchen. An older man sat at the table while her aunt leaned against the counter. "Oh, good," Lucy said. "You're up."

Grace did not smile or react.

The old man looked at her through rheumy gray eyes. He was wearing a thin plaid shirt that hung off his bony frame and dark blue trousers that appeared to be cinched around his waist with a wide brown belt. His cheeks were sunken, but his eyes were kind.

Grace turned to Lucy. "I need to talk to you."

Lucy nodded. "All right."

Grace glanced back at the old man. "In private, please."

Lucy stood straight and placed her hand lightly on the man's shoulder before following Grace out of the room. "What is it?" she asked as they entered the living room.

Grace pushed her hair back from her face and kept her hands in her hair. "I need you to tell me what's going on now." Her voice wobbled when she spoke in not much more than a whisper.

Lucy looked at Grace in that careful way, but Grace didn't want that anymore. She didn't want *careful*. She wanted the truth.

"Your mom brought you here so that you could rest." Lucy's voice was calm and even.

"And why do I need to rest?"

Lucy didn't answer.

"I've been having these dreams—" Grace stopped herself. "Dreams that aren't dreams."

"What are they then?"

Grace lifted her shoulders then blew out a breath. "They're—I think they might be real."

Lucy stood, silent, while Grace pushed her fingers harder into her hair. "I know it sounds crazy, but when I woke up, I could have sworn that I'd actually been there."

"Where?" Lucy asked.

"I was with my father. We were in a restaurant…" Grace trailed off as she struggled to recall all of the details of the scene. And before that—her friends, the test. It had all been real, but now it seemed to be disappearing from her mind like a trail of smoke slipping through her fingertips. "There was a little girl," Grace said. "Her name was Lucy." She held onto that detail.

"It's not that common of a name, I guess," Lucy said, and smiled. "But you are here with me, so is it that unusual that you would dream about me?"

"You don't understand. It wasn't about you. It was him. My dad. He wanted me to come and live with him."

Lucy still just looked at Grace patiently. Grace sank onto the arm of the sofa and leaned her elbows on her knees, resting her head in her hands. "Something isn't right," she said with certainty. She felt Lucy's touch on her back, making a small slow circle.

"He said that you were dead," Grace said through her hands.

Lucy's hand stopped, and they were both still for just a moment. Grace waited.

But all Lucy said was, "It's going to be okay." She took a breath. "Come and let me introduce you."

The old man, Grace remembered. "I don't want to meet anyone right now. I just want to go home." She missed her bed and her friends and her life. She missed

Brandon. She even missed her mother. And she didn't want to be in this strange place with these strange people.

Lucy patted her back twice and went back to the kitchen, leaving Grace alone in the small sitting room. Grace sat there for a few moments. What was she supposed to do? She was trapped, stuck, alone. There was no one to listen to her. She felt infinitely sorry for herself.

She sighed before she followed her aunt back to the kitchen, where the old man sat in the same position he'd been in before. She wanted to lash out in anger, but that wouldn't do any good. None of these people even had a vehicle to drive her out of here.

If Lucy noticed Grace's anger, she didn't comment. Instead, she said, "I'd like you to meet Henry," said Lucy. "Henry, this is Grace."

Henry looked at her and gave a small nod. Lucy did the same. Neither of them smiled or spoke, but they sized each other up through lowered eyelids.

Lucy had made some sort of fragrant tea out of herbs and served in old, chipped mugs. "Henry stops by every and brings me some supplies. He keeps an eye on things so I can get out of this place for a bit."

Grace looked sideways at Henry. "Where do you go?" she asked Lucy. "Can I come with you?"

"I thought you and Henry could spend some time together."

The last thing that Grace wanted to do was spend time with this old man. "When will you be back?"

Lucy smiled at her. "Soon." Then she walked out the back door.

Grace blew out a breath, feeling alone, confused, angry, scared. Most negative feelings applied to her at that moment.

Henry shifted in his chair, took a long swallow of tea, and spoke for the first time. "We can do a bit of fishing after you get yourself some breakfast."

Grace looked at the long lanky fingers with their paper-thin skin wrapped around the mug in front of him. She stood and stared out the window, trying to see which way had Lucy walked into the woods. But there was no sign of her.

"How do you know Lucy?" she asked.

"I've known Lucy for a long time."

Grace didn't point out that his response didn't answer her question, but she was getting kind of tired of all her questions being answered in riddles and plays on her original words.

"Do you live close to here?"

"Yes," he answered.

"Do you have a car?"

He chuckled. "I used to have a truck. That was a long time ago."

"Now you just walk everywhere?"

"Something like that."

Grace sighed. It was going to be a long afternoon. She buttered some bread and gobbled it down before she turned around to him again. "What do I need to go fishing?" She was getting comfortable with just surrendering. She could not make any choices for herself at home, and it was more of the same here.

"Just yourself. I'll bring the rest." He stood and rinsed out his chipped teacup.

Grace looked down at her t-shirt and shorts that she'd been wearing since the beginning of her stay. She was sure that her hair was matted, tangled, and probably pretty oily by now. The only mirror, the one above the sink, was chipped and warped. It didn't give her much to go on. But she didn't *feel* grimy or dirty. And even if she did, she didn't think this old man would care. "Do I need to change?"

"Nope." He walked out the back door. "I'll meet you down at the river," he called over his shoulder.

Grace thought about just going back to bed and sleeping the rest of the day away. Would she be able to go back to her old life if she fell back to sleep? But part of her didn't want to disappoint Lucy for some reason, although she sometimes went out of her way to disappoint her mother.

Besides, if she went back to sleep, she'd just have another bizarre and corporeal dream, and she was getting confused about what was real and what wasn't.

With resignation, she slipped on her sneakers that

were sitting near the door and walked down to the water's edge where Henry was standing with an ancient-looking rowboat that looked like it would immediately take on water. "Is that yours?" she asked doubtfully.

"I've been known to use it."

Grace eyed it. "Is it safe?"

"You know how to swim." It wasn't a question.

"That doesn't make me feel very secure. But, yes, I do." She'd been on the swim team at school for years. She'd quit in the middle of the season in her Junior year, much to her mother's dismay. Part of the plan had been for Grace to get a swimming scholarship to at least a Division-Two college or university—like Megan.

Grace, though, had grown tired of the time alone in the water. She hated the early mornings and the afternoon practices. She hated the regular meets and the relentless pursuit of fractions of seconds. She hated constantly competing with herself to be even better.

At least, that's what she'd told herself. Away from it all, she could admit that part of it was the lack of time she'd had to spend with Brandon and her new friends. While Brandon understood the commitment because of his own athletic pursuits, she had been almost desperate to be with him. Swimming was cramping her style.

She helped Henry push the boat in the water, and after sloshing through the ankle-deep rush, she stepped into the boat. Henry stepped in after her, taking the back seat.

"Is it deep enough to move?" she asked as they drifted toward the rapids. She took the paddle from the seat beside her and glanced back so that she was in sync with the old man.

"We'll be fine," he called back over the noise of the rapids. They scraped bottom once or twice, but once they reached the other side of the river, the water deepened, and they let the current take them downstream, using the oars only to steer.

Grace looked up at the sky. The morning had started as a steely gray with soaking rain, but there were breaks in the clouds where a brilliant blue showed through. It was warm but not hot, and a breeze fluttered her hair. She breathed in the smell of the river—the smell of earth and water, then she let out a great breath. A sense of relief flow through her as the sun warmed her face.

Henry didn't talk as they floated on the water, and Grace watched a hawk soaring high above them.

After about twenty minutes, she felt some movement behind her and watched as Henry threw down a small anchor that had been sitting beside him. "This is deep enough," he announced and handed her an ancient-looking fishing pole and a small container of dirt and worms. "You've been fishing before."

Some deep part of her mind was activated, and she

had the slightest memory of something very close to this. Who had she been fishing with? It must have been her father. Whatever she was remembering, though, wasn't quite the same. She remembered red clay and sitting on a bank while someone beside her cast into the water.

Grace knew what to do. She knew how to fasten the bobber onto the line. She knew how to pinch a wriggling fat worm onto the hook. It didn't make her squeamish as she'd thought it would. She cast to one side as Henry cast to the other in the middle of the river that didn't seem to be moving nearly as swiftly now. She could still feel the pull on the rope attached to the anchor.

They sat quietly for a few minutes, and then Grace broke the silence. "You said you've known Lucy for a long time. Does that mean you knew my mother, too?

He paused for a few seconds. "I knew Mariah well."

"But not anymore."

"Once you know someone, you always know them, in your heart."

"I don't think she's ever mentioned you."

He smiled. "No, she wouldn't have."

Grace reeled her line in slowly, a little closer to the boat. She rested the rod on the bow. There was a lot her mother had kept from her. And she felt the same about Lucy, though, with Lucy, it was different. With Lucy, it felt like she was waiting for Grace to figure it out on her own.

"There's a lot Lucy isn't telling me," Grace announced.

Henry's hands were steady as he reeled his line in and examined the hook where the worm had been a few minutes earlier.

"What do you want Lucy to tell you?"

"Why I'm here, for one thing. My mother dropped me off and didn't even say goodbye." Grace sighed. "Lucy said that she brought me here because I needed to rest, but I've been having these bizarre dreams." She stared at the slow ripples the pull of their boat was making in the water. "I'm not getting any rest at all."

She hadn't expected Henry to answer, but he did. "Sometimes, the rest you need is not for your body, but your soul."

She was quiet.

"Look around you," he said, and she glanced up from the water to the deep green foliage of the trees bending toward the river. "There's a feast for the senses right here where you are."

Grace felt the slight breeze on her face, smelled the rich, silted earth so strong that she could almost taste it. The water lapped easily against the boat, and birdsong sounded from the hidden nests.

"When is the last time," Henry asked, "that you sat still long enough to notice where you were?"

"I don't know," Grace responded. She wasn't sure

she even knew what he was asking.

"Your mother was a lot like you when she was a girl."

Grace looked back at Henry, who had his eyes fixed on a point in the distance. He leaned his rod against the side of the boat and took a curved pipe from his chest pocket, filled it with a pinch of tobacco from a small pouch that had come out of the same pocket. The smoke was sweet and rich, and another memory tickled the back of Grace's mind.

"How was she like me?"

"She was always thinking, but with that same twinkle in her eye. Like she was trying to find a way to trip you up while you were talking to her." He chuckled. "It's no wonder she became a lawyer."

Grace smiled. "She can get anything out of anybody. And you don't even know she's doing it."

Henry laughed. "When she was a little girl, probably five, she got me to admit that Santa Claus wasn't real. Then she told Lucy, and Lucy was devastated. Cried for two days straight." He shook his head. "But it was my fault, falling for her tricks. She always was too smart for her own good."

"It sounds like she was something else."

"Oh, she was. Still is. Successful and smart. And she made you, and that's pretty special."

Grace colored. "I'm nothing like her at all. I have no idea what I'm doing." She thought about the SATs and knew that she had taken them and had done poorly. She knew that that hadn't been a dream but a memory of an experience in which she hadn't participated fully.

"Mariah always could talk a good game. That's how she fools other people. And that's how she fooled herself."

"What do you mean?"

"What you see as confidence is often fear. Mariah has built a successful career and makes a lot more money than she needs, but she's constantly afraid that's all going to come crashing down around her. The way it did when she was young. She's afraid of being vulnerable. That's why she pushes you. She knows that you have abilities and opportunities that she didn't. And she doesn't want to see you waste those."

Grace stared at the old man, who was reeling in his line. "Lost my worm," he muttered. She watched him dig into the dirt and grab another wriggling worm, who didn't have a choice, and spear it with the sharp hook. She could relate to that worm.

"How do you know all this about her?"

"About Mariah? I told you—I've known her a long time."

"But I've never seen you, and she's never mentioned you. You aren't a part of our lives."

Henry cast the line and sat quietly, staring off into the distance. Grace thought he wouldn't answer and opened her mouth to continue the interrogation when Henry spoke. "It was a long time ago before you were born. And I've kept tabs on her over the years. From a distance, I've watched her grow and learn, and I've watched her be a mother to you."

"You stalk us or something?"

He laughed. "Nothing like that." Then he considered. "Maybe a little like that. But it's hard to explain."

Grace opened her mouth, then felt a persistent tug on her line, which was now stretched taut. "I think I got something," she exclaimed.

"Reel it in, girl!" Henry leaned forward. He watched, but he didn't offer to help her.

She pulled back slightly and wound in the line, careful not to tug too hard and dislodge the fish from its precarious hold. She worked this way for a few minutes, pulling firmly and in a controlled way and then reeling consistently.

"You got 'em," Henry yelled, and Grace felt the perspiration run down the sides of her face and neck.

It put up a good fight, but a fat trout was on the end of it when the line emerged from the water.

Henry helped grab the fish and deftly removed the flapping creature from the hook, where the worm still wriggled. He threw it into an old cooler he'd brought with him. "Looks like we'll be eating well tonight."

Grace laughed and wiped her face, which shone with sweat from the sun, effort, and excitement. It had felt natural to pull that fish in, and she knew that she'd done it before but couldn't remember when or how.

"Let's see if we can't get us another one before we head back," Henry said, and Grace agreed.

They recast their lines and sat quietly for a while. Grace was tempted to ask about Mariah again and Henry's connection to her, but she didn't want to ruin the moment. The sun sparkled off the water's surface. She looked over at Henry, and he smiled at her. "You're doing okay," he said, and his words made her feel good. She let out a breath.

Henry caught another fish, with just as much excitement as Grace's earlier conquest. Afterward, they made their way upstream to their launch point, where they dragged the canoe out of the water together. Grace carried the cooler and the poles while Henry maneuvered the canoe back to Lucy's house.

Lucy was on the porch sitting in the old wicker rocking chair and stroking Logi when Grace came up the overgrown driveway.

"How'd you do?" Lucy asked.

"We got two big ones for dinner."

"I knew you'd like going out with Henry. He's a heck of a fisherman."

Lucy waved at Henry as he pulled the canoe to the back of the house, then set Logi on the ground and met Grace to take the cooler from her. "I'll take these out back. Henry will want to clean them."

Grace hesitated, then asked, "How does Henry know me?"

"Henry's a part of the family, Grace."

As Lucy walked down the porch steps and around the house, Grace followed. "He said that he watches Mariah."

"Henry cares very much for Mariah, and he cares very much for you. He just wants to make sure you're both doing okay."

"The more time I spent with him, the more familiar he seemed to me." Part of Grace thought that she might have gone fishing with Henry before. But she knew that would have been impossible.

She and Lucy reached the back of the house, where Lucy placed the cooler beside an old wooden picnic table. Henry emerged from beside an outbuilding against which he'd leaned the old rowboat.

"Henry," Lucy called. "Grace thinks she may be starting to remember you."

Grace colored and narrowed her eyes at Lucy, who didn't seem to notice.

But Henry's face brightened as he walked toward her. "Do you, now?" he asked. "What do you remember?"

Grace shrugged. "You just feel... familiar. I feel like I may have done all this before. You seem like someone I've always known."

"To tell you the truth, I wasn't sure you'd remember. You were so small."

"Then we did spend time together?"

"When you were just a wee one."

"Where?" she asked. "And why?"

Henry laid a hand on her shoulder. It was the first time he'd touched her. "Here," he said quietly. "Grace, I'm your grandfather."

# CHAPTER SIX

G race opened her eyes in her own bedroom. She lay flat on her back, wearing the clothes she'd worn to the school that morning. She stared at the ceiling for a minute, trying to get her bearings. She felt like she was losing her grip on reality. The dreams were extremely real. Lucy and Henry. She struggled to keep them close so that she could ask her mother about them.

She looked over and saw her phone on her nightstand and picked it up. She had a message from Brandon asking where she was and was about to reply when she heard raised voices from somewhere in the house. She set the phone back down and pushed herself up on her elbows.

She heard her mother say, "We need to get her to the hospital," and then a lower voice in response, but Grace couldn't make out the words.

She stood up quickly, and the blood rushed to her head, making her woozy. Maybe there really was something medically wrong with her.

She grabbed the phone from the dresser and sent

Brandon a message back. "I won't be too much longer."

She immediately got a message back of Jessica making a pouting face.

Her blood turned to ice and pooled in her stomach. Now, Jessica had Brandon's phone? Grace stared at it, thinking about how she wanted to respond. But the raised voices continued. She threw the phone on her bed and made her way to the door—one problem at a time.

"She's been acting strangely for two weeks now, Scott." Her mother's voice cut through the space in the townhouse. "You wouldn't know because you chose to move two hours away."

"It wasn't my choice, Mariah. I have other people to consider now." As usual, her father was playing defense in the conversation.

"Yes, your other family. The one that matters. You don't think Grace feels that? And right now, we're talking about Grace. But as usual, you want to turn it around and make it about you. You're such a *victim*." The last word was spat with such venom that even Grace cringed.

The hazy words of Henry came back to her—the old man calmly explaining that her mother's confidence was often fear. Could that be true? Grace held her hand to her head as she made her way down the stairs slowly, holding onto the banister as she went.

They both looked over and up at her, startled, as

she entered their field of vision. They stared at her for a minute as if she were a ghost, then rushed over.

"You're up," her mother said, meeting her halfway down the staircase and laying a cool hand on her cheek as she walked Grace down.

Her father stood at the bottom, awkwardly waiting with his hands in his pockets.

"What happened?" she asked. "Why are you here?" It came out as more accusatory than she intended, but it was a shock to see him in their home. He'd never stepped foot inside the front door.

"You fainted," he said. "Just went right down in the restaurant."

Grace closed her eyes as her mother guided her to the sofa. Right now, she was feeling as if she were living in two separate realities. Her mind was cotton, and she shook her head. But she remembered the restaurant. She remembered sitting there with her father. She opened her eyes and looked at him. She remembered what he'd asked her to do.

"I'll get you some water," Mariah said, walking briskly into the kitchen.

Her dad sat down next to her. "I'm sorry. I may have sprung too much on you. About our conversation. If you could just forget about that for now, until I have a chance to talk with your mom." He kept his voice low.

Her mother came back with a glass of water, and

Grace took it and drank.

"What's happening with you?" Mariah asked, staring at her intently.

Grace looked back at her dully, too tired and confused to be intimidated or pressured into answering. The truth was, she had no idea how to answer her mother's question.

"Is it stress? I think it might be stress." Mariah didn't wait for a response. "Maybe now that your SATs are over, you can slow down and relax a little bit."

Grace remembered how poorly she'd done on the tests. She thought maybe she had blacked out then, too. She decided not to bring that up.

"We'll take you for some tests now," her mother said with finality.

"No," Grace said quickly. "I'm fine. I was just tired."

"Did you sleep last night?"

Grace thought back to the night before, which seemed like ages ago. She thought of the strange dreams and the strange people, who weren't strangers at all.

"Tell me about Lucy."

Mariah's face lost its color, and a white line appeared around her lips.

Her father said quietly, almost under his breath, "She asked about Lucy earlier too." It was almost imperceptible, but Mariah straightened and pulled herself together so quickly that you would have thought the brief loss of composure had never happened. Her thin hand brushed a piece of her short, sleek auburn hair behind her ear, and she inhaled deeply. "Why are you asking about Lucy now?"

Grace detected the slight tremor in her mother's voice, and it was only because she felt like she'd been shown another side of this woman.

"I think I have a right to know. She is my aunt, after all."

Mariah hesitated, then said, "She was my sister. She died. There isn't much more to tell."

Grace's heart thudded in her chest. Dream or not, the memories of Lucy were very real. To hear her mother say that Lucy was dead changed things somehow. Made it more final and infinitely more perplexing. And it scared the hell out of Grace.

"How did she die?" Grace had to ask the question.

"It was a long time ago, and it doesn't matter. And it has nothing not do with the matter at hand, which is you, and your health. You blacked out in a restaurant, Grace. You could have hit your head. And there could be underlying issues. We need to get you checked out at a hospital."

"Did Lucy have an accident?"

Mariah's look could have caused a houseplant to wither.

Her father picked it up. "This really isn't the time—"

Grace sliced her hand through the air between them. "Really isn't the time for what?" she yelled. "To tell me the truth? I've been alive for seventeen years, and I've barely even heard her name spoken. Who *does* that? Who keeps an entire family history a secret?"

"It's not a secret," Mariah answered. "It's simply not relevant."

"Why do you get to make that choice for me?" Grace asked. She snorted slightly. There had been a lot in Mariah's life that Grace suspected had shaped her mother's personality. This was most likely one of those things.

"Scott, go get her something to eat. There is peanut butter and jam in the cupboard. Something with some fat and sugar." Without question, her father rose from the chair and started toward the kitchen.

Her mother turned back to Grace. "You're going to eat, and then I'm taking you to the hospital."

"Forget it," Grace said and stood up. She wobbled a bit but corrected quickly. "I'm not eating, and I'm not going to the hospital."

Her father had stopped midway to the kitchen. "Your mother is right, Grace. You need to—"

"You've always done that, haven't you?" Grace asked.

He knitted his eyebrows. "I'm not sure—"

"You've always just agreed with her. Whatever she told you to do, or however she told you to behave. Do you do that with Shannon now?"

His mouth fell open, and Mariah was now standing. "That is enough!"

"She's even fighting *this* battle for you. With your *daughter*." Grace turned toward her mother. "And you're really going to defend him? After all of the horrible comments you've made about both him and about Shannon?"

Her father looked like he'd been slapped, but still, he didn't speak. Mariah's mouth was an angry slash. She started to say something. Grace cut her off. Her focus shifted back to her father. "Why don't you tell her what you asked me to do?" she dared her father.

Now, he looked horrified. "This isn't the time."

"Then when is the time? Are you going to wait until I make a decision and then blame me, either way? Is this all even your idea, or is it Shannon's?" Grace had nothing against Scott's wife. She was nice enough. A little bland, though she went out of her way to make Grace comfortable when she visited their house. But it would never be Grace's home.

Mariah's attention turned from Grace to her ex-husband. Her eyes narrowed slightly. "Scott, tell me what Grace is talking about."

At least she'd forgotten about the peanut butter and the hospital.

"It's nothing," he said weakly. "It's not worth discussing right now."

"It sounds as if it's worth a conversation." Mariah's voice was cool and calm. She was fully in possession of her wits and the direction of this discussion.

Her father sputtered. "But Grace..." He motioned helplessly toward her. "We have to get her checked."

"You didn't even want to take her ten minutes ago," Mariah countered.

Grace knew that if her dad could have been successful in just running out the door, he would have done just that. He may have been a lawyer, but he preferred to pen his opinions. The guy would have never been able to cut it in oral arguments.

She felt bad for him, but it hadn't been fair of him to ambush her with his ridiculous idea, dump it in her lap and make her deal with it. She may have done that before, but not now. Too many things had gone unspoken in this family.

Her father looked at her, and she shrugged. "This is the conversation you should have had first."

"What did you say to her, Scott?" her mother demanded.

"I..." He ran a hand through his thinning dark hair. "I asked her to move in with us."

Mariah laughed. "Why on earth would she want to do that?" She looked at Grace.

Grace didn't speak but looked back at her father.

"I thought it might be good for her for a year. You know, get away to a small town, make some new friends."

"Because that's what every high school senior wants to do. Make new friends a year before leaving and doing it all over again."

"I just thought—"

"That you would have a built-in babysitter when you have your next child." Mariah shook her head. "Ridiculous plan." She may as well have waved him out of her existence, so complete was her dismissal.

Her father looked angry. "You have no idea what I thought. You don't know now, and you didn't know when we were married. You are always completely sure of yourself, and sure you know what's best for everyone around you. Other people have their own thoughts and opinions, you know."

"And who usually turns out to be right in the end?"

"Are you really that arrogant? You don't even bother to listen."

"I don't need to listen to this. There is no way Grace wants to live with you."

Mariah was correct, but no one ever turned to her to verify.

"It's not even about Grace. You were positive that you knew what was best for me and my career. You were sure you knew what kind of father I needed to be and what kind of man I should act like." His face was red, and his eyes bulged. He caught sight of Grace in his periphery, still standing behind the sofa. "I'm sorry,

Grace," he said. "We shouldn't be doing this in front of you."

"Grace needs to know what kind of person you are." Mariah lifted a shoulder. "You're weak. I thought I could make you stronger, but just look at you now. Floating a completely impossible plan because your new wife told you that's what you should do. And bringing up the past because it's a direct mirror of the present."

Her father looked like he might implode, and Grace went to him. "Dad, just go. I'll call you later."

"I'm sorry, Grace."

"Don't apologize. It's fine, and I'm fine."

After he'd walked out the door, Grace stared at her mother, who had shut her eyes. When Mariah opened them, she reset her face and began walking toward the kitchen. "Okay, the sandwich." She had switched gears completely.

"Mom, I'm not eating the sandwich. And I'm not going to the hospital."

"Yes, Grace. You are. You passed out. Something is wrong."

"How can you just dismiss him like that?"

Mariah was silent for a long time. "Your father... He's—He means well most of the time. But he's impotent. He's incapable of making a decision for himself or of moving forward without someone moving for him. There was a time that I thought I could fix that about him. I *wanted* to. But then it just became me making all of the moves for him."

Grace thought about that. She thought about her mother making all of the moves for her lately—because that's what was happening. Was Grace letting it happen? Was it just easier that way? She was tired of trying to be the perfect daughter for this woman who would mold her into the creation of her choosing if Grace let it happen. "I bombed the SATs," she blurted out, just to get a reaction.

Her mother turned slowly. Then she smiled as if Grace had just made a joke. She wagged her finger. "Your future is not something to joke about, Grace."

"I'm not joking. I blanked. I didn't even finish the test."

Mariah stood silently for a second. "You're serious." It was half question, half realization that she didn't want to hear.

"I took the prep class, I took the practice tests, I studied the flashcards. They did not help me."

Mariah looked stricken, raised her hands to her hair, and then dropped them. "These tests are how you get into the right school. You know that, right?" Her voice was stern, but Grace could detect a hint of panic behind the words. "I told you that you had to keep your head on straight, get enough sleep, and eat properly." She let out a breath. "Maybe if you were still swimming—"

"I'd be even more exhausted than I am right now," Grace exclaimed, finishing her mother's thought with her own.

"You'd be even more *structured*," Mariah corrected. "You know, Grace, I can't walk you through your life. You have to want things for yourself."

"And if the things that I want aren't the things you want for me? Like the things you wanted for Dad were not the things he wanted for himself?"

Mariah had clearly decided to ignore the quip about her ex-husband. "How could you possibly even know what you want? You're not even trying to figure it out. You're not looking at schools. Your grades slipped last semester. And now, this news about your SATs? What in the world is going on with you?"

Grace looked down. She marveled at her mother's ability to shift from utter concern about her wellbeing to a lecture on how she wasn't trying hard enough. Maybe she *should* just go to live with her father and Shannon.

The thought flashed in her mind suddenly, and her head swam for a minute while a hot bolt stabbed the pit of her stomach. She could not leave her friends. She could not leave Brandon.

Brandon.

She'd forgotten him for a second. The images from Jessica's story appeared to her once again.

"I have to go," she said abruptly.

Mariah stared at her. "Go where?" she asked, bewildered. Then she said, "You're not going anywhere. Out of the question."

"I have to go to see Brandon."

"Grace," her mother began and exhaled, trying a new approach. "I know that life seems overwhelming right now, but you'll get through it. You really will. Forget about Brandon and your father right now. Forget about school and your grades and swimming. You're here, and you're safe." Her eyes were gentle for a minute as she lay a hand on Grace's shoulder.

It was such a dramatic shift in the conversation that Grace thought she'd imagined it.

"If you don't want to go to the hospital, fine. It sounds like this is all self-induced, stress-induced. Eat something and rest today. I will be home later tonight, and we can talk more then. And we will figure something out."

Grace knew that the "we" in the sentence wasn't actually plural. It meant that Mariah would figure something out on her own and then loop Grace into the solution. In fact, Mariah would probably be building this solution throughout the day, and when they spoke later, it would just be easier for Grace to agree and go along with the plan than to fight back. She felt paralyzed right now, so she threw out another verbal bomb. "And maybe we can talk more about Lucy."

Mariah shook her head, walked toward the stairs. "There is nothing to talk about, Grace. I've told you that, and I'll continue to tell you that. You need to go to your room and rest."

"How did she die?"

Her mother stared straight at her. "She killed herself. And I don't want that for you."

# CHAPTER SEVEN

G race opened her eyes and looked around. The sight of the full bookshelves was a comfort in the fading light of day, and she breathed in and out the slightly musty scent of old wood and clean earth. She was on the sofa in the cabin in the woods. It was as if a switch had been flipped, and depending on the blink, she had no idea in which reality she would appear.

As she was becoming much more conscious of the shift, the images faded quickly.

Lucy smiled at her from the armchair as if nothing at all was amiss. Grace pressed her hand against the sofa's rough fabric, which was solid and real against her palm. She looked around, imprinting the sur-roundings of her present reality. She was definitely here, right now, just as she'd been in her home with her parents. A dream? A memory? It was hard to tell. Already the images were fading into wisps of thoughts.

"Why can't I just remember?" Grace wondered aloud.

Lucy considered this. "Do you know how, some-times, you know something deep down in your soul, but you just aren't able to admit it to yourself because it would cause too big of an adjustment in your life?"

Grace shook her head. She felt a slight pressure just behind her eyes. She was tired of talking about all of this.

Lucy tried again. "When your parents divorced. After they told you, and when you thought back on it, weren't there signs that you thought you probably should have recognized?"

When they'd divorced, she had been seven. She did remember arguments; her father, sleeping on the sofa when she would come down to watch cartoons early in the morning. She remembered the kitten that he'd brought home. It had been gone the next day. She vaguely remembered crying over it, but it had soon been forgotten, with no name to recall. She remembered eating dinner with her mother but couldn't remember a time that they'd all sat at the long kitchen table in their previous house outside of the city.

Had signs existed that her parents' marriage had been distressed? She supposed so. But it was distant to her.

"The last thing I remember my mother saying to me in this last *dream-slash-memory* was that you killed yourself. If it's a memory, is that true?"

Lucy looked past Grace toward the window, where the trees were bending over the front porch in the strong breeze. Logi jumped up on the sofa and settled in the crook beside Grace's left hip, and his purring vibrated her whole body.

Lucy seemed to be weighing something. Then she asked, "Do I look dead to you, my dear?"

Grace didn't answer. Of course, her aunt didn't look dead. She was right here. Grace could feel her energy as sure as she could feel that cat beside her and the cushion beneath her.

"And Henry is my grandfather?"

"He is."

"He is my mother's father. He is your father."

Lucy nodded.

Grace shook her head. "I don't buy it. She wouldn't lie to me about something like that. She may hide behind silence, but when confronted, she speaks the truth, always. Even when it would be kinder and easier to lie." It was one of the things that Grace both loved and hated about her mother.

"It's not that simple, Grace. We've always been here, yes. But Mariah has dealt with the circumstances of her life in her own way, and she was never able to return to this place."

"But she brought me here."

"She did, yes. And for that, I am grateful. Someday you will be, too."

"But did it surprise you?"

Lucy considered that. "When I found out she was coming with you, yes. Your mom can be...hard, and she rarely admits when she was wrong."

Grace put her hand on her head. "I don't know what to do."

"Well, the good news is, you don't have to do anything right now."

Logi purred more vigorously against her side as if he sensed her distress and could erase it, or distract it, with his energy. She reached over and stroked his soft fur.

"I can't just sit here," Grace said. "I can't just stay here. I have to try to get home if my mother isn't going to come for me. Does Henry have a car? He said that he kept tabs on us. He must know where we live and how to get there."

Lucy smiled sadly. "I'd love nothing more than to be able to take you back there, but it isn't time."

"You keep saying that, but I have to figure out what happened and why she hates me. Why they all hate me."

"Oh, Grace. There is only love for you."

"I saw my mother's face when she dropped me off. It wasn't filled with love."

"You don't know your mother well."

"I've known her all of my life. She's tough and independent and unbreakable." Grace paused and then said in a small voice, "I think I may have done something to break her."

Lucy patted Grace's hand and stood. "We all do

things that we regret; sometimes they're big things, and sometimes they're small things. But there are no mistakes, Grace. Whatever happened had to happen, and you deal with it the way you deal with it. You can let it change you, but you can't let it define you. Because if you do, you're going to have a really sad time in the time that you have on this earth." She shrugged slightly. "And then, what would be the point, really?"

She walked out of the room then, leaving Grace to stare after her, with no idea what Lucy was talking about.

✝ ✝ ✝

After a time, Grace stood slowly and found that she felt fine. Her headache was gone. She gave Logi one final pat and walked outside to the front porch. The day had turned gray again. No rain fell, but the air was hot and heavy, a dismal blanket settling over the land. Even the birds weren't singing. The land was perfectly still and quiet. Even the sound of the river was muted.

Grace stepped off of the front porch and walked down the overgrown driveway. She hadn't seen Henry since they'd come back from the fishing trip, which seemed like earlier this morning, but at the same time, felt a very long time ago.

She turned back and looked at the small house. The

place did seem familiar, as if she'd been here before, a lifetime ago. She had many questions that should have simple answers. And yet, those answers eluded her.

Why had her mother told her that Lucy had killed herself? How in the world was it possible that Henry, who apparently was her grandfather, was still alive and Grace hadn't, in recent memory, met or seen him?

None of this made any sense, and Grace was getting a very bad feeling that she wasn't ready to acknowledge yet.

She wrapped her arms around her midsection and walked to the end of the driveway, then she looked left and right at the remnants of the road that traversed the wood. She could see nothing but trees and shrubs and greenery in either direction, and she turned to her right and started walking.

A few hundred feet past Lucy's house, the vegetation grew denser, and the path disappeared altogether. A humid mist hung low over the scrubby vegetation. Tall trees created a natural ceiling, and the day was even darker than before. She felt as if she were in a haunted forest populated with gnomes and spirits.

Grace glanced behind her as she walked and wondered what would happen if she lost her way. Would she die out here in the forest? Starve? Eat some poison berries and lie moaning for days where no one would find her? Or would some tiny woodland creatures band together to take her to an enchanted cottage in the wood?

She kept walking, tempting fate. Daring the universe to take her and swallow her whole. Daring it to show her what was next.

Eventually, she came upon a clearing in the woods that was littered with some trash. The spell was broken. Beer bottles and empty bags of potato chips sat beside a few downed logs that looked like they'd been placed in a haphazard circle. Grace looked around. No one was here now, but clearly, there was other life nearby, or at the very least, a way that humans rather than fairytale creatures had accessed the area.

As she was scanning the area for a path, she heard a noise that made her stop. It was a low humming, not animal, but human. Someone was humming a tuneless song. She looked around and saw some movement through the trees toward the river.

She moved closer cautiously until she came upon a very real man. He sat, legs spread, on a downed stump, not far from the riverbank. His head was bent forward, and his arms were both moving smoothly on a task that she couldn't quite make out. He didn't seem to notice her, and she moved carefully to her left, trying to make out his movements. Then she could see that he used a large knife to skin the bark off a branch.

A break in the clouds appeared, and one brief shaft of light burst forth and danced off the water. The sudden brightness caused Grace's hand to move inadvertently to shade her eyes, and the man seemed to notice her movement. He turned and looked at her, seeming surprised to find someone in his existence, but not shocked that she had shown up suddenly.

"Hi there," he said in a mild, low voice.

"Hi," Grace said tentatively.

This man was lean, with a scruffy beard, and Grace could not tell how old he might be. There were lines around his eyes, but his smile was full and open. However, Grace was very aware that she was in the middle of nowhere with a stranger, who could very easily overpower her. And this was a much different concern than one of spirits and woodland fairies.

He made no attempt to approach her or even get up. He just continued to whittle the long branch. She relaxed a bit and was about to turn around and return from whence she'd come when the man asked, "What brings you out this way?" He glanced at her quickly, then moved his focus back to his task.

"Just taking a walk."

"Don't see too many people out here."

She motioned back to the clearing. "There's garbage back there. People must come here."

He furrowed his brow. "Kids come down from town every once in a while. Usually up to no good. But they don't come during the day. This isn't a great fishing or swimming spot, and there's not much else to do around here anymore."

"Anymore?"

"When I was a kid, there were six or seven houses down here. It wasn't exactly a town, but we had a community. Then everyone left."

"But you still live here?"

He nodded.

"You know Lucy?"

He didn't look up, but his whittling slowed. "Lucy. Yeah, I know her."

"I'm her niece."

He stopped what he was doing and turned to look at her. "You're Grace," he said and smiled. He studied her for a minute longer. "You look like her, you know. When she was your age. Pretty little thing. Wouldn't have expected you to be staying with her." He nodded again, then went back to his carving.

"Why is that?"

He shrugged. "This is a quiet place. We don't get too many visitors. Unless they need to be here."

Grace listened to the steady swish of the knife's blade against the limb.

"What are you doing?" she asked, as she watched the gray wood peel from the branch to reveal new white skin, tinged with green.

He held up the branch. "Making a bow for hunting. You want to get the young limbs so that they bend and stay flexible."

"What are you hunting?"

"Whatever I can. I had a really good and sturdy bow, but age snapped it a while ago. Figured it's about time to make a new one."

Again, Grace wondered if she should feel nervous. But there was no point, she supposed. No one was looking for her; no one cared where she was.

The look on her mother's face when she'd left Grace in that overgrown driveway... Terror, wrath, desperation. She was never coming back.

"And you knew my mother?"

He smiled, and his face lit. "Mariah. Yes, I knew her well."

Was it her imagination, or did his voice possess a certain wistfulness? "But not anymore," she clarified.

"Does anyone really know her now? Hell, I don't think she even knows herself."

Grace thought about Lucy's earlier words to the same effect. She thought it was odd that this man would pick up that theme, too. And odder still that would mention her mother in the present as if he'd had contact with her recently.

"Do you know *yourself*?" she asked. She wasn't trying to be cheeky, but all this talk of knowing oneself. Grace had no idea how you were supposed to get to that point or what it even meant.

He looked up and narrowed his eyes. She'd thought maybe she had offended him, but then he laughed. "Good point," he said, pointing the knife in her direction. "You're smart, just like your mother and your aunt."

Grace was a little bewildered. "I wasn't asking to be funny," she said. "I was just asking."

He was still chuckling. "I know myself now," he said, "but it took me a long time to get there."

The scraping of the knife against wood continued, and she realized that she didn't like watching the bark of the tree curling to the ground and discarded as if it had never really mattered at all. As if it hadn't been there for protection. She was watching one form take on another form—same material, completely different use.

"So...who are you?" Grace asked.

"Jon," he said and nodded his head once at her.

"And you've known my mother since she was a child?"

"I met your mother when I moved in with my grandparents. She'd have been about eleven at the time, I suppose. I was thirteen."

"Where were your parents?"

"They were around. I'd gotten in some trouble— nothing major—but they thought it would be good for me to get away from the kids that I'd been calling my friends."

"Kind of like me."

Jon flicked his gaze in her direction. "Is that why you're here?"

"I'm not sure. No one will tell me, and I'm having a hard time remembering."

He nodded, then continued. "We caught the school bus at the end of the road." He pointed in the direction from which Grace had come. "There were just the three of us—Mariah, Lucy, and me. Couldn't help but know each other."

Grace found it hard to believe that school transportation would come this far outside of civilization. "Can you tell me about her?" she asked Jon.

"What is it that you want to know?"

She thought about that. "People keep telling me that I'm like her. Or at least, I'm like her when she was young, but I don't know what that means. Was she smart, was she driven, was she funny, was she depressed, did she love a boy, what did she want to be when she grew up?" Grace took a breath. "All of those things."

"That's a lot of things," he said, chuckling. "And, yes. To all of them. And she'd wanted to be a dancer when she grew up. A ballerina."

She thought about her mother, tiny and lithe, with the perfect bone structure. Grace could have imagined her as a dancer, and yet she'd never seen her dance. She had, however, watched her listen to classical music and close her eyes. She wondered if her mother was dancing in her head.

"You saw her dance?"

"A few times. She took lessons in town. She was pretty serious about it back then and not as reserved as she is now. She would dance down the lane when she was younger."

Again, the incredulity. His description was completely out of character with the woman Grace knew. But why would this man lie to her?

"Were you the boy that she loved?" she asked, instead.

He was quiet. During his silence, Grace noticed that the branch had a gentle curve to it, and Jon handled it gently.

"At the time, yes, she believed she loved me."

"Did you love her?"

He smiled. "I was a teenaged boy, but at the time, yes, I believed I loved her, too."

How was it that she was sitting with her with her mother's first real love, maybe her *only* real love, and yet the subject had never come up? Did her father know that Mariah had loved someone before him? Grace felt sad for her mother, keeping these stories and feelings bottled in always. And she felt sad for herself.

"What happened?" Grace asked.

Jon shrugged. "Nothing really happened. She went away to college."

"And you stayed here?"

"I stayed here for a while after she'd gone. I left for a time but found my way back again."

Grace looked around them. She saw now a discernable path to a home, and she saw no evidence of a house through the trees.

He followed her gaze and gave a just of his neck toward the sloping hillside. "I live in a house just through those trees."

"Maybe she would have come back if she knew you were here."

He chuckled and shook his head. "Mariah never wanted to stay in one spot. She wanted to move, she wanted to dance, and she wanted to explore things outside of our tiny world." He gestured to the trees above him and around him, and to the river. "I always found great beauty here, where things were quiet."

"And still," Grace said.

"You think they're still until *you* become very still. Then you hear dozens of unique birdsongs, see the rustling of the leaves and limbs all around you, feel the unceasing wind on your face. The movement never stops. Mariah could never still herself long enough to understand that." He smiled a little sadly. "But that's okay. That's who she was. That's who she still is."

Grace thought about her mother, who indeed never slowed down. There was work always. There was the unstoppable nervous energy that made Grace feel like she, too, could never slow. There was endless planning and movement.

"She was the opposite of Lucy, I take it."

Jon's movements slowed. "Lucy," he said a little reverently. "She was something else entirely."

Grace noted the past tense use of the name. "You don't see her? You live right down the—" She paused, looking at the barely existent path from which she'd traveled. "She lives right over there," she tried again.

"We encounter each other from time to time," he said. "Lucy and Mariah are in different places now than they were way back then. Mariah was the ocean—expansive, undulating, overwhelming, impossible to miss—Lucy was a deep lake hidden in the trees. Once you found her, you never wanted to leave. She had borders, but her depth was immeasurable."

He had loved Lucy too, Grace realized. Could that be the reason Mariah never talked to Grace about her aunt?

He stood from the stump on which he'd been sitting, and she noticed that he was tall. Much taller than her father. Leaner and weathered.

He came closer to her, and she backed away. But he just looked down at her. "You have a little of both of them in you." He gathered up his wood and knife. "I have to go back and check on my girls if you'll excuse me."

"Girls?" Grace asked.

"Sophie and Anna."

For some reason, this shocked her. "Are you married?" she asked.

"You could say that." He started walking, and Grace followed him. He didn't seem to mind.

"Is your wife here, too?"

"Not yet."

"Where is she?"

"You have a lot of questions."

They walked out of the trees and up a slight slope into a meadow. When Grace turned to her right, she could see where a road once was. It looked like there were some fresh tire tracks on the grass, and she wondered if this is how Jon came and went. She didn't ask. He'd never answered her question about his wife.

Instead, he said, "So long, Miss Grace," and winked in her direction.

She watched him go, but she didn't follow him, this strange man who knew both her mother and her aunt and lived in the thick of the woods. She heard the crack of a stick and looked away for a second. When she looked back toward the direction that Jon had walked, he was gone.

# CHAPTER EIGHT

G race had no trouble finding her way back to the cabin. In fact, it seemed that no matter which way she turned in the dense woods, she was guided back to where she needed to be, even when she had no idea herself.

Jon had said that the forest was alive with sounds and sights, and she recognized that as she walked. In addition to the multitude of bird calls, there was also the incessant and comforting sound of the river and the rapids, keeping her grounded, reminding her that she was where she needed to be. It was a strange sensation of complete belonging in this world around her. Compared to a world where she had always felt...other.

She had shut her eyes a few times and felt the overwhelming urge to cry, and yet she wasn't sure why. She hadn't been upset or worried or angry or frustrated. She had never felt surer of herself in her life.

When the cabin came into view suddenly as if it has been dropped right in her path, she walked up to the front door. All of the memories of earlier came flooding back to her. The conversation with Lucy about her death, the need to escape home.

She took a breath before going in. The urgent need to leave had left her, and while she still wanted answers, they didn't seem quite as urgent now.

She walked into the cabin, and neither Lucy nor Logi were in the small space.

As the light was fading outside, she randomly pulled a thick text off of the shelf, still marveling at the collection in front of her. Where had Lucy gotten all of these books? Who had brought them?

She opened to a random page of the fat draft in her hand. A poem leapt off of the page and into her consciousness.

### Eternity by William Blake

*He who binds himself to a joy*
*Does the winged life destroy*
*He who kisses the joy as it flies*
*Lives in Eternity's sunrise*

Mrs. Morrison, her English teacher, had assigned a poem by Blake earlier in the year, but she didn't remember much significance about it. She read this short verse again and savored each of the words.

If you attach yourself too tightly to a thing, object, or person, you will destroy your life, Grace thought. "Winged life." *Fleeting life.* If Grace had discovered anything, it was that life was impermanent. However, if you appreciate the joy as it comes to you and the thing, object or person leaves again, you will "live in Eternity's sunrise." Sunrise was the youngest part of the day, where new life and fresh beginnings existed. Is that what the poem meant? If you could appreciate what was in front of you in the present moment, you would not be overwhelmed by life's grief?

It was a great concept, Grace supposed. It would be nice if that was the way that things worked. But she knew that it wasn't just about the appreciation for the beautiful things. There was a lot of ugliness in the world.

She sank down on the sofa, looking through more pages, waiting for Lucy to come home so she could ask her about Jon. She knew there was a story there, and it encompassed both Lucy and her mother, and Grace wanted to know what it was.

She read another of Blake's short verses, this one about love, which made her think of Brandon. Did she love Brandon? She desperately believed that she did. She missed him and would give anything to talk to him. To have him put his long, lean, and muscular arms around her and just hold her close.

She threw the volume onto the sofa more violently than the book itself deserved and went to the small bedroom that she was calling hers for the time being.

She had not finished her junior year classes. She

had not finished her SATs. How was she supposed to go to college next year if she hadn't finished her junior year? How was she going to make up the time, the tests?

She knew that there was still time, but she would be behind, and she hated to be behind. She wanted everything to work out just as she had planned. Spending god-knew-how-long in the wilderness was not a part of her plan.

She picked up her phone. Completely dead and useless. She sighed heavily.

The light was disappearing by the second. She had to get out of this place and get back to her real life. She understood the need to rest. She understood that her mother hadn't wanted to see her, but that didn't mean Brandon hadn't wanted to see her. She had to get back to him.

Was Jessica with him right now? Were they laughing at her?

Grace thrust herself from the bed and nearly ran down the stairs and out the front door. There was no way that she was going to let that bitch Jessica have what belonged to her. She had to get back home. Now.

She ran out the door and into the shadows of the wilderness, toward the river. With a moment's hesitation, she decided to follow the water downstream. Water always knew where to flow.

She hurried along the bank in the twilight, the light

of the sun somewhere behind the clouds setting somewhere far beyond the trees. She was probably walking north right now. Was that the direction she needed to go? How would she know without any knowledge of her current location?

A fresh wave of anger at everyone in her life. Including Lucy and Henry. *Henry…* Where had he gone? He'd just disappeared like everyone else seemed to in this godforsaken place.

She heard the hoot of what sounded like an owl in the distance.

Something rustled in the brush beside the riverbank and Grace kept her eyes forward. She hadn't considered the unfamiliar wildlife that she might encounter. Coyotes and foxes lived in the forest outside of the city. She'd even heard about reports of brown bears near her town. Why wouldn't they be in these woods as well?

As the light continued to dwindle, the smells of the forest became more intense. The river was muddy and earthy. Rich and dirty. It was familiar to her here.

She kept walking, resisting the urge to turn around and run back to the cabin.

Soon, the last vestiges of illumination were gone from her atmosphere. It was a moonless night, and without even a fading light to guide her, she walked in deep shadows. She tripped over foliage and low limbs, and branches like tiny hands pawed at her as she passed, trying to hold her back or extract something from her.

The river still flowed, and she followed its rushing toward an unknown destination.

She crashed hard into a stump, bruising a shin, but caught herself before she fell.

She thought about Brandon as she walked, trying to get back to him. He was her beacon, her light in the darkness. His smile kept her going, and she fixed that image in her mind as she walked blindly.

Something seemed to growl low and angry, extremely near to her. The image of Brandon faded, and her blood turned to ice. One side of her body erupted in prickles that warned of danger.

She let out an inexorable whimper, and then she began to run.

Her eyes had adjusted to the shadows illuminated in front of her, and she lifted her legs high to avoid tripping, at the same time expecting to hit hard into an invisible object. The sound of the river kept her steady, but she started to cry. She could see Brandon's face in front of her, radiant and real. It seemed she could almost reach out and touch him.

*Brandon.*

*Brandon.*

*Brandon.*

Her feet hit the ground in time with his name.

Then her shoe caught on something, some ground

vine or rock, and she went down hard. Then she started to tumble, faster and uncontrollably, toward the rushing water. She didn't have time to try to stop herself or brace herself for the impact of icy and brackish water. She didn't have time to process the thoughts as they flew toward her. She was falling.

☦ ☦ ☦

Grace's eyes flew open, and she felt damp with perspiration. Her breaths were great gulps of air, greedy and insatiable. With some effort, she forced herself to slow her respiration, counting off seconds as she breathed in—two, three, four—and out—two, three, four. She repeated this cycle a few times until she felt solid, and the cobwebs began to clear her head.

She looked around her bedroom and experienced a vague sense of coming here to wait until her mother had left the house again. There had been a fight with her father about her. About her going to live with him. About his motivation.

She knew that her mother had dinner plans with Peter, a swank reception with the Mayor. Grace could not have imagined that Mariah would have missed that to stay home and play nursemaid to Grace. No matter how worried she was about her daughter.

Grace glanced at her phone. No messages for her, but lots of pictures from her friends on their stories.

Pictures of Brandon and Jessica.

She stood up quickly, felt woozy, and grabbed the bedpost.

*An image—the forest, the river, falling... falling.*

She swiped a hand over her face, breathed out deeply. She did not have time for any more of this garbage. She needed to stay in the present moment. She couldn't afford to have any more of the nonsensical dreams that had been plaguing her. They made absolutely no sense. And even if they had, no one was willing to answer her questions about them. She needed to stay on solid ground and in her right mind.

She stood at the door to her bedroom, listening for sounds coming from the rest of the house. She detected no noise at all. Mariah was probably, right now, dressing at Peter's, telling him what a disappointment Grace was turning out to be.

And Peter, who was ten years older than her mother, was probably nodding sympathetically, if distractedly because he had absolutely no interest in getting to know Grace. He was more concerned with his cars and his house, his reputation, his money.

They would both be dressed to the nines, Mariah in her slim emerald cocktail dress and impeccably matched jewelry, elegant and intimidating with her beauty and her wit. Peter in a sharp tuxedo, his silver hair slicked back from his handsome and smooth face. Quite a pretty picture they'd make, and Grace would probably be able to see them online, in the About Town column in the Style section of the city's online newspaper.

Grace went into her bathroom and splashed cold water on her face. She gazed at her reflection in the mirror. Shadows darkened her hazel eyes, and her cheeks and lips held no color. Her hair looked mousey and flat. She pulled her hair up into a high bun, mussing it up until long blond tendrils fell around her face. Then she dabbed on some concealer, blush, and lip-gloss.

Better. But she was nowhere close to the high-gloss stature of her friends. Or her mother, for that matter. She was plain Jane compared to all of them.

She was pretty, she supposed. But boring. A wisp of a girl who was neither interesting nor intriguing. She wouldn't stand out at all in a room.

There was no question why Brandon was hanging out with Jessica.

She went into her bedroom and pulled on a bathing suit. Two-piece. Skimpy. Something she'd bought last summer on one of her first shopping trips with Alyssa when the friendship had still been new. Alyssa had squealed in delight when Grace had held it up, and Grace had purchased it, even though she could never imagine wearing it. She had been used to her one-piece team practice suits—practical and substantial. But here she was, finally with a reason to wear the thing, and it was to get Brandon back.

She regarded herself in the full-length mirror on the back of her bedroom door.

She had strong shoulders, and a full chest, a flat stomach, and muscular legs. She was a little more solid than Jessica or Alyssa from the years of swimming. The bikini looked good, though. She was fairly certain that no one would notice the dark circles. Not the boys anyway.

The party would be well-attended. Nate lived in one of the most upscale neighborhoods north of the city, where people with new money had settled in sprawling McMansions and perfectly manicured lawns. Nate's father was an executive vice president at a cyber-security company. Nate had mentioned it a few times in terms of money. Everything with her friends was in terms of money. And even though Grace's mother hadn't made as much money as many of her friends' parents—mostly fathers—Mariah was the most publicly high-profile of the group. Her job required frequent interaction with the press, and the high-profile cases she often prosecuted gained her a lot of attention. Grace had been accepted as one of the elite.

Grace had been to Nate's house before. It had a pool—heated, almost half indoors. Real potted tropical foliage surrounded the pool-scape, making you feel like you were somewhere else—on vacation in a Caribbean resort. While she hadn't been swimming during her last visit, she had marveled at the faux beauty.

Grace threw some casual clothes on over her swim-suit, grabbed a small purse and her phone, and climbed into her small red car, which was parked on the street in front of the house. After her episode at the restau-rant, she assumed her father had driven her home. He had most likely driven her car here and then took a ride service back to the restaurant to pick up his own car.

It was unseasonably warm for a late spring day, and the interior of her car was hot. She sat in the driver's seat and let the car run with the air conditioning on blast.

The car's speakers had automatically paired with the last music streaming service, and a folk song played from the last playlist she'd been listening to. The song illuminated in glowing green letters on the digital screen on her dash: *I believed you, William Blake.*

A finger of anxiety, cold and uncomfortable, ran down her neck, causing her to shiver. She, of course, knew who William Blake was. They'd had to read *The Songs of Innocence* earlier this school year in her Advanced English Literature class. But there was a more recent memory of William Blake, and she couldn't quite place her finger on it.

The memory/dream of Lucy came back, and she tried to put shape to those wispy ruminations that escaped the trap of her mind.

Another snatch of memory overtook her, quick and strong. A scruffy man who had known her mother. A man who had known Lucy. A man walking slowly away from her in the woods.

As if on cue, the music was interrupted by an incoming call from her mother.

Grace answered the call on her phone rather than through the car's speakers.

"Gracie, how are you feeling?" Mariah asked.

Her mother's use of her childhood nickname meant that she was feeling guilty for leaving Grace. Her father used the same name when he called to cancel their visits.

"I'm fine."

"Are you sure? I can come home if you need me to."

There was a part of Grace that wanted to call her bluff. Would she really miss her gala, or whatever it was, if Grace asked her to? She thought about it for two beats. But Grace had her own party to attend. "No, that's okay," she said.

"Well…" Mariah's voice faded away. In relief, Grace thought. No need to feel guilty if Grace told her it was okay. "There is some cold chicken in the refrigerator if you get hungry. Or order pizza if you'd like."

"Did you know someone named Jon?"

Silence.

"Mom?"

"Yes, I'm here. Grace, why would you ask me something like that?"

"Then, you didn't know anyone named Jon?"

There was an audible sigh. "I've known lots of people with that name. It's a common name."

It was an artful way not to answer the question. "When you were young," Grace clarified, needlessly, she knew.

There was another pause, and she could tell that Mariah had gone into another room of Peter's house. Peter must have been listening to the conversation. "I'm not sure how you could have possibly known about him," Mariah said quietly.

"Who is he?" Grace asked.

"It's not a big deal," Mariah prefaced. "He was my high-school boyfriend."

"What happened to him?"

"I haven't the faintest idea."

Grace knew that her mother was lying by the general consideration of the question. If she hadn't known, she wouldn't have entertained the question at all.

"Why are you asking me about Jon? Why have you been asking about Lucy?"

Grace did not want to tell her because it sounded crazy. You simply did not just conjure people from your parent's past in the middle of vivid dreams. Dreams that came randomly during blackouts in the middle of the day. Lucy and Henry were one thing. She could have heard about them in snippets of conversation. She could have found an old photograph. Her grandmother could have randomly mentioned them during a visit.

But a high-school boyfriend? That was reaching.

"Did you find something?" Mariah asked carefully. "A letter or diary…?" Her words trailed off. There was a pause, then her mother said, "Or an old yearbook. I can't imagine there is anything… It was so long ago. Maybe something online…" Her voice had a very faraway quality—contemplative, reflective.

"You don't know where he is now?"

The pause was longer this time. When her mother spoke again, she sounded tired. "Grace, you really need to get some rest, okay? I—I have to get ready. I'll be home later, though, and we can talk through all of this—your father, Lucy, Henry. Jon," she said quietly.

"Okay," Grace said, satisfied that maybe she would get some clarity about her strange visions after all.

She was about to press end when her mother said, "I love you."

Shocked, Grace mumbled, "You too," as she disconnected. Of course, she knew that her mother loved her. It just wasn't often that the emotion was verbalized. Grace found herself shivering.

# CHAPTER NINE

Nate lived only a few miles away from Grace, but on a Saturday mid-afternoon on the busy two-lane highway to his house, the road was clogged with traffic. Where was everyone going, Grace wondered. What could they all need so desperately at these arbitrary stores crowded together like the urban version of a foreign marketplace? Pet stores, craft stores, restaurants, clothing outlets, beauty suppliers, booksellers, camping outfitters. Did people really need this much *stuff*? she thought.

As she navigated the start-stop traffic, Grace's head began to pound, and she started to think her mother may have been right. Maybe she should have stayed put at her house. Though the air conditioner of the car blasted against her face and neck, she felt slightly feverish, unnaturally warm where she should have been cool.

A popular country song played through her speakers, and for some reason, it made her want to gag. She switched off the audio system and drove in silence.

She squinted at the brake lights in front of her and

watched, strangely detached, as cars pulled in and out of the businesses on each side of the road. She drove slowly, aware of her limitations. Was it the early heat? Was it the stress, as her mother had said? Was it the strange dreams or the lack of restful sleep? Could there really be something wrong with her? Could she be sick? Maybe she should have let her parents take her for the tests.

If nothing else, it would have forced them to spend some time together. But what would that have accomplished? They certainly were not going to get back together.

It would have been nice for them to care for her, together, or even for their love to be more about her than about their own issues.

The red lights of a pickup truck appeared suddenly in front of her, and she slammed on her brakes. She braced for an impact that didn't come. She breathed heavily, her heart in her throat. A vehicle came around from behind her, the driver laying on its horn. The man gestured crudely as he came up beside her and swerved in front of her car.

She tried to concentrate on the road in front of her, but still, the scene played out like a dream. For a second, she couldn't remember how to get to Nate's and heat prickled in her armpits.

She focused. She needed to make a left past the high school, she thought deliberately. She had some time before she had to switch lanes, but because she was unsure, she moved over into the left lane immediately, eliciting another angry honk from a driver she had cut off. She gripped the steering wheel tightly.

Her phone buzzed, and she glanced down to see a snap from Alyssa.

*Where R U?*

She was disappointed not to have heard from Brandon.

Even though she knew she shouldn't, she took her chances and, one-handed, typed back to Alyssa, *On my way.* She swerved slightly into the other lane and then corrected quickly. She went back to gripping the steering wheel.

Grace made it the rest of the way to Nate's opulent home, halfway down a street lined with other impressive structures. As she pulled into the circular driveway, scattered with other new and expensive cars, she stared up at what could only be described as a mansion. A local sports hero lived two doors down, and the guy next door had founded and then sold a popular fast-food restaurant that was now franchised across the country.

When Grace had first started hanging out with this group of friends, these homes used to impress her. Now they seemed a bit unnecessary. Who needed this much room? Who needed this much house for a family of four?

She parked at an angle in line with the other cars—there must have been at least fifteen—all more expensive than her sensible make and model, then sat for a moment in the quiet of her car. Her head was still pounding, but she no longer felt like she was going to throw up. She shut her eyes for a minute in silence, willing herself to feel better.

A man who appeared to live on the other side of the house walked down the length of his lawn, staring disapprovingly at the haphazard collection of vehicles. Grace watched him, and then he caught her eye, shaking his head slowly as he walked to his mailbox and retrieved some papers from the ornate wrought-iron structure.

He walked back up his driveway, alternating between glancing at the mail and shooting disapproving looks in her general direction.

She waited until he went inside his house, then walked to the front door. The heat hit her as she walked, and she felt woozy again. When she got to the door, she rested her forehead against the cool metal, then straightened and raised her hand to knock. When she heard the loud bass of heavy music emanating from someplace inside, she simply opened the door.

A growing sense of foreboding rose to meet her. She wasn't sure why. These were her friends; this was her crowd. She'd been to parties before with these people.

The artificial coolness of the air conditioning hit her like a wall, and she sank down on the stairs, boisterous voices rising from somewhere in the bowels of the house to meet her. She shut her eyes and slumped against the wood, smelling of lemon and oil, new and old. And she let the darkness envelop her.

☦ ☦ ☦

"There she is."

The male voice sounded faraway, slightly out of focus, then came closer to her.

"How long you think she's been out here?"

"Hard to tell. Not that it matters, I guess."

"Thinking it's going to matter to her some."

Grace's eyes fluttered open, and she was staring up into bright sunlight. The loamy smell of the river assaulted her nose as she took a gasping breath.

The two men's faces peering down at her were upside down—both tan, weathered by the elements. She struggled to sit up.

"Easy there," one of the faces said, putting a steadying hand behind her back. Both men came down to a crouch in front of her.

She squinted for a second longer, then she recognized Henry and Jon, peering back at her, close.

"Where am I?" she asked.

"Looks as though you're on the bank of the river,"

Henry answered.

"I mean, how did I get here?"

Jon held out a water canteen, and without thinking too much about it, Grace drank it down. As she gulped, the younger man said, "It looks like you fell asleep right here on the bank."

She handed the canteen back and muttered her thanks. "I was running—" She stopped short of saying that she was running away. "I tripped, I think. I fell."

Henry stood and looked from Grace's spot on the muddy bank to the water rushing just a few feet away. "I guess you're good and lucky you didn't fall in and float away."

She thought maybe that might have been better. At least she would have gotten somewhere, even if it had been just her body.

Jon offered her a hand, which she took and hoisted herself up. "What time is it?" she asked.

Neither of them answered at first. Then Jon glanced up at the sun starting to rise high over the opposite bank. "Must be about ten."

Grace looked from one man to the other. "Were you out here together?"

"Suppose we were," Henry answered.

"Come on," Jon said, interrupting her line of questioning. "Let's get you back."

She figured that they'd be walking miles back to the house. She had walked for a long time last evening and into the night. It had taken her hours before she fell. But as they made their way up the bank and down the pathway, she realized they weren't more than a few thousands yards from the cabin's front door. She felt completely foolish.

Lucy was at the front door waiting. She didn't look anxious or worried, but her brow was furrowed in what appeared to be a mild disappointment.

"You are as stubborn as your mother," she said, taking Grace's hand and leading her inside to the kitchen table.

Logi was sitting on the tabletop watching Grace with his amber eyes.

Lucy poured Grace another glass of water from the spring pitcher and set it down in front of Grace. She drank it without being told.

Henry was moving around the kitchen like he belonged, but Jon was standing awkwardly in the doorway. A flash of conversation with her mother floated lazily into her mind as she looked at Jon. She said to him, "My mother told me you were her boyfriend."

Lucy asked sharply, "She said that?" Then her voice softened. "Well, of all the wonders."

Jon seemed surprised, too.

"Getting Mariah to admit something to herself once she has it in her mind—even a cold, hard fact—is like teaching a dog to read."

Logi looked at Henry, and Henry said to the cat, "Don't get offended. She said *dog.*" Then Henry turned his rheumy gaze on Lucy. "I told you she wasn't that far gone. She wouldn't have brought Grace here if she was."

Grace asked quietly of Lucy, "Was Jon your boyfriend, too?

Lucy was quiet for a minute. "What do you think, Jon?" she asked, her back to him. "Is that what we were all those years ago?"

Before he could answer, two small but powerful voices came tumbling together into the house, followed by two small girls and two small kittens.

Lucy clapped her hands together, delighted and distracted away from Jon and the question of their relationship. "Kittens," Lucy exclaimed, moving forward and scooping one of them up in her arms. One of the kittens was coal black with long fluffy fur, and the other was white with large green eyes that held a vast intelligence. They both looked happy to have been found.

"They followed us here," the smaller of the two girls piped up.

"They live with us now," the slightly larger girl said definitively.

"Oh, do they?" asked Jon, but he was laughing.

"This one is Lily," the littlest girl said.

"And this one is Rosemary, like mommy," the other girl said.

Jon said, "Mommy will like that. But what if they are boys?" The girls looked highly unconcerned with the gender of their new pets.

The little girls noticed Grace, who seemed to hold as much interest to them as the animals. "Who are you?" they asked in unison.

"Sophie, Anna, this is Grace," Jon said, and both little ones held out their hands for her to shake. The gesture was such an adult one, and the incongruence made Grace feel awkward. Like she was the small child in this situation, instead of the other way around.

"Nice to meet you," Grace said.

"How did you get here?" Sophie asked. She was the larger of the two, with the wild dark hair and big, intense hazel eyes.

Grace was a little taken aback by the question, and she sputtered. How exactly was she to answer that question when she didn't know the answer herself. "Well... My mom brought me here, I guess."

Anna said, "Our Mommy asked us to stay here with Daddy while she stayed back."

Grace frowned. "I thought your home was through the woods."

Before Anna could speak again, Jon said, "Okay, girls. Enough questions from all of you. Grace has had a tumble, and she needs to rest."

Anna clearly didn't think this applied to her. She

came very close to Grace and touched her long hair, which was probably filled with mud and leaves from lying on the riverbank all night. Anna's hair was a brownish color made a coppery-red by the sun. She had a sprinkling of freckles across her nose, giving her an impish glow. Her eyes weren't as intense as her sister's, but they held just as much intelligence and a bit more humor. She seemed much older than a little girl should have been. "Your mom probably wanted you to keep Miss Lucy company. Or maybe miss Lucy is here to keep *you* company."

Grace lifted half of her mouth in a sort of smile. The black kitten leapt around her ankles, chasing something—some invisible insect. Logi was uninterested in the new kittens and instead regarded Grace carefully.

Sophie picked up the white kitten, who purred so loudly that Grace could hear it from across the room.

"Is that Lily?" Grace asked.

Sophie rubbed her cheek across the kitten's small head. "I actually think this one might be a boy," she said.

Grace laughed. "How can you tell?"

"He might have told me."

"You can talk to animals?" Grace hadn't meant for the words to sound derisive, but she was aware of the skepticism in her voice.

"You can talk to anyone if you know how to listen,"

Sophie said.

Henry let out a whooping laugh. "Ain't that the truth," he chuckled.

Grace moved closer to Sophie and leaned down, putting her ear closer to the cat. This little girl seemed to know something that no one else in the kitchen knew, and Grace wanted to know how she knew it.

"You don't listen with your ears," Sophie said.

Anna nodded solemnly.

"How do you listen then?" Grace asked. She stared at the little kitten in his green eyes. A flash of recognition met her, and she jerked her head back.

Sophie laughed. "Just like that," she said. "With your heart. Or your soul. And then you'll just know."

Jon leaned down then and scooped Anna up into his arms, and she giggled. "Come on, monkey."

"I'm not a monkey," she yelled, laughing. "I'm an elf."

Henry said, "I thought you were a fairy."

"Last week, I was a fairy. This week I'm an elf."

"Sounds reasonable." He turned to Sophie. "What about you, little one?"

She considered this. "I'm the wind today."

Grace shivered even though it was humid in the kitchen, crowded with all of these bodies.

Sophie turned her gaze on Grace. "You're still a girl."

"Well, yes," Grace said. This spooky little thing was

giving her the creeps. "And so are you. And so is Anna. And so is Lucy."

"Lucy is the light."

"That's what her name means," Grace responded.

Jon said again, "Come on, Soph. Let's leave Miss Lucy, and Miss Grace be for now."

Sophie stared at Grace, then lowered her eyes to the white kitten. "This is Brandon," she said, and Grace's voice shook when she said, "What did you say?"

Sophie peered at her under thick eyelashes, fixed her with a steady gaze, and then turned to her father. "I'm ready, Daddy."

Jon nodded, tipped his head at Henry, and said to Lucy, "Good to see you again."

She smiled up at him. "Thank you for coming."

"Happy to be of assistance. Grace," he said, nodding. "See you around, I expect."

Still unsure how to react to any of what had just happened, she simply raised her hand.

When they had walked out the door and taken their kittens with them, Logi jumped from the table and disappeared himself. Henry came over and kissed the top of Grace's head. "Take care of yourself."

"Where are you going?"

"I'll be around," he said, echoing Jon's words. Henry fluffed her hair and said, "Just like your mother." Then he chuckled and walked out the back door. She heard him say something to the chickens. Then he was gone.

Grace hadn't wanted to face Lucy alone. She felt like she'd disappointed her aunt by trying to get back home. "I'm sorry—" she began, but Lucy's bemused expression stopped her.

She said, "You don't have to be sorry for wanting to go home."

"It's not that I don't like spending time with you," Grace said, weary to her bones. "It's just that this isn't the place that I'm supposed to be."

Lucy sat across from Grace. "There's no sense in wishing you're somewhere else."

"I thought if I just followed the river…" Grace's words trailed off.

"If you follow the river, you'll make it somewhere, but it won't take you home."

Grace nodded, and Lucy continued, "If it means anything to you, I don't think you belong here either. At least not forever. But your mother, for her own reasons, wanted you to come here and learn some things about yourself. And maybe she wanted you to teach her some things about herself." Lucy lifted a shoulder, exuding radiance, as always. "Things for Mariah didn't turn out the way she had expected despite all of her planning. Your mother will try to shoehorn life into a custom-made mold and then wonder why her soul has blisters all the time."

"Is that what happened with Jon?"

"Jon was probably the love of her life. But when she was young, she was looking for something else, something better. And Jon was—well, he was full of life. Real life, not just the possibility of it. She never shared this with me, but I would guess that Jon overwhelmed Mariah and made her feel something that scared her or made her feel vulnerable. Your mother likes to feel in control. And she went off to college and met someone she could control."

Grace imagined that her dad would have seemed mild compared to the slightly wild and earthy Jon.

"But he was the love of your life, too?"

She didn't hesitate. "Yes."

"And then something happened, and he over-whelmed you, too?"

"I overwhelmed myself." Lucy stared into the distance for a minute, thinking, remembering. She smiled, and it was filled with light and joy. "I forgot that you can't hold onto an experience. You can only appreciate it and be thankful that you had it in the first place."

Grace thought of the poem by Blake.

Lucy continued, "That's a hard lesson to learn when you're young. If you're like Mariah, you may never learn it at all. And if you're like me, by the time you need to learn it, it's too late."

Grace said, "I haven't had to learn it yet."

Lucy reached out and touched a warm palm to her cheek. "Oh, Gracie. That's why you're here."

# CHAPTER TEN

G race filled the small, rough bathtub slowly with a
stream of water from some well that must have
existed deep under the earth somewhere, then
submerged herself. The chipped enamel was a far cry
from the gleaming white marble of the townhome she
shared with her mother. Even her father's older home
was more updated than this shabby house. But
something here felt comfortable, like a well-worn pair
of slippers or an old fuzzy robe when you were home
sick from school.

She sank into the water and let it wash over her
long hair while she stared up at the water-stained
ceiling.

She could breathe here.

She thought about her friends, who seemed farther
than ever from her. What had Alyssa wanted to do
with her life? Did she want to be a teacher or a doctor
or a nurse? Grace was sure they'd never discussed it.

And Jessica, the thought of whom filled Grace with
a sense of uneasiness. Jessica had specifically said that
she didn't want to work for a living. She'd wanted to

marry well and marry rich and spend her free time traveling and enjoying life. Whatever that meant. Grace was sure that Jessica hadn't shared any specific goals, like children or philanthropy or animals. She seemed only concerned with herself. Grace hadn't remembered that troubling her before, but now she questioned why she hung out with Jessica at all. What was she gaining from that relationship?

An agitated part of her knew that the answer to that question was popularity, which Grace would never have gotten from her swim team friends. Jessica was sleek, gorgeous, and easily the most recognizable girl in school. And Grace was her friend. Or *had been* her friend.

Thoughts of Brandon came back. That little girl telling her that the kitten's name was Brandon. It had to have been a coincidence, of course. Grace was beginning to feel more and more disconnected from her life at home. She wondered if that existence even intersected with this one at all.

She sighed, let herself fall back under the water, looked through the distorted view at the ceiling. She held her breath until she felt like her lungs would burst.

She came up, sputtering, then stood abruptly, sloshing water over the side of the tub. She pulled the old-style plug out of the drain, and the water was sucked into the house's piping network.

She dried off with a stiff and threadbare towel, then

looked in the fogged and dingy mirror that showed another distorted image of herself. It wasn't even possible to recognize the girl in the reflection.

Grace walked to her room and pulled on a fresh set of clothing set out by Lucy. Then she walked downstairs and saw Lucy working in her garden at the back of the house. She appeared to be expanding the garden's footprint and was working soil that had not yet been planted.

When Grace walked outside, the chickens clucked over to her and pecked at the ground around her feet.

"Feeling better?" Lucy asked.

Grace nodded.

"You look just like Mariah in those clothes."

"Were they hers?"

Lucy leaned against the hoe. "They probably started out as mine, and then Mariah got them. There wasn't a lot of money for clothes back then."

Grace had never had to experience a lack of sufficient money. She looked around and knew that *this* was why. This early life that her mother had lived. "Why did you live way out here?" Grace asked Lucy.

Lucy started hacking away at the rich soil again. "Henry worked on the railroad. At the time, this small village was close for him and affordable. And it wasn't as lonely back at that time. There were houses here, even a little post office."

Grace sat on the back steps and leaned forward.

"What happened?"

"People moved away, and there wasn't a market here for the houses. There were no jobs here anymore. The coal mines were gone, the railroad wasn't carrying as much freight. The houses fell into disrepair and were either torn down or rotted away."

"But you stayed."

Lucy nodded. "This place is in my bones."

Grace considered the familiar and comforting sounds and the solitude. She could understand the pull for Lucy. But Grace still longed to be around people. She didn't think she could live her life this way.

"It's not in my mother's bones."

"I think some people can surprise themselves withwhere they go back when wounds need to be tended."

Lucy made her way down the length of the tilled soil, dropping in bulbs like they were something precious. She was quiet as she continued her gardening.

Grace stood and went into the house. She buttered a piece of bread and ate it, more because she thought she needed the sustenance. She was, in fact, not hungry at all. She hadn't been hungry since she'd arrived here.

She chewed and noticed Logi watching her from his spot on the table. She felt as if he were specifically observing her, and it unsettled her, much like the little girls of Jon had disturbed her with their quiet, watchful eyes and self-assuredness.

She walked past him into the living area and sat down on the moth-bitten armchair. She shut her eyes for just a second, and when she opened them again, Logi had silently moved into the area and curled up on the sofa. Still, he watched through half-closed eyes. Too tired to shoo him away, Grace slept.

✝ ✝ ✝

Grace woke up to someone yelling, "I think she's already drunk!"

Eli and Nate were standing at the front of a group of kids—some of whom she recognized and some she did not. She stood too quickly from the steps where she'd sat and shut her eyes after feeling dizzy. "I'm not drunk," she insisted, then her knees buckled, and she caught herself against the banister as the blackness rushed in from both sides of her eyes. "I'm just not feeling well."

Nate guffawed, but Eli leaned closer. "Are you okay?" he asked as Nate lost interest and walked to a room near the back of the house, where the music was coming from.

She nodded as her senses came back to her, and her vision cleared. She took a deep breath. "I haven't been feeling well all day," she said. And she absolutely didn't feel like being at a loud party, but she was desperate to see Brandon.

Eli took her elbow. "You aren't high, are you?" he asked cautiously.

She shook her head.

When he seemed certain she wasn't going to fall, he motioned her to follow him. "Everyone is out back."

She followed him to the back patio, where a group of at least thirty bodies undulated in various states of undress to loud music around the large pool. Two senior girls from her gym class were splashing around in the pool, with two older boys that Grace knew had graduated last year. Their bikinis were nothing but scraps of material barely covering their breasts. She looked away, sure that by the end of the night, there would be plenty of nudity.

Two kegs stood off in a corner against the house, and a group of mostly boys was gathered around them. Red plastic cups littered every surface, even standing sentinel in the potted plants. There didn't seem to be much ownership of the drinks.

Someone thrust a cup filled with liquid into Grace's hand without any other sort of greeting. No one was happy to see her or appeared to be waiting for her. This party had devolved into oblivion quite some time ago. Grace frowned, but she held onto the drink as she scanned the crowd for Brandon.

She found him quickly across the length of the pool, close to the hot tub, which was raised up on a platform. He was naked from the waist up and wore a pair of light blue swimming trunks. His lean torso was deeply tanned. Grace immediately noted that Jessica, clad in a similarly extra small bikini, was standing extremely close to his side. She wasn't touching him, but that didn't matter. She was staring up at him, batting her long eyelashes, leaning in close.

Brandon did not seem to be the least bit uncomfortable with this specialized attention. In fact, he was smiling down at her with a glint in his eyes that Grace didn't think she'd ever seen before, even from this distance. He leaned forward and whispered something into her ear.

Her stomach lurched, and without thinking, she gulped down the liquid in the plastic cup. It wasn't beer, and she sputtered on the straight vodka, her throat burning and eyes watering.

A boy named Tanner, who was only in a few of her classes, had watched her, and he yelled, "Hardcore!"

She took a few breaths, composing herself and breathing through the fire in her throat and the lump in her chest. She was aware of a distant cheer, but her full attention was on Brandon and Jessica on the other side of the swimming pool, and they hadn't looked away from each other once.

It only took a few seconds for the first effects of the alcohol to dull the edges of her awareness, and a fuzziness surrounded her as she walked. Even though she knew her unsteadiness had less to do with her impairment than it did with the other events from today, it probably did very much appear to the rest of the partygoers that she was already drunk.

When Brandon caught sight of her, he straightened and leaned away from Jessica, who saw her at the same time and leaned closer to him.

Brandon did not smile, but Jessica did. "There she is," she said smoothly as Grace approached. "Don't worry," she continued, the long tips of her fingers touching Brandon's bare stomach. "I've been keeping him warm for you."

Grace ignored her.

Brandon said, "Hi, Grace," without meeting her eyes.

While she hadn't been angry about the lack of contact throughout the day, it all came rushing back to her now. He hadn't snapped or called. He'd only texted once, to which Jessica had replied to her response. She'd been through a hellish conversation with her father, more than one with her mother, and not to mention the blackouts. And where had he been? Slobbering over another girl, while Grace had been the furthest thing from his mind.

But she didn't say any of these things. Instead, she forced her expression neutral and her voice casual and asked, "How's the party?"

"It's okay. Fine."

She consciously took a smaller sip of her the vodka and looked around. Three girls were giggling in the deep end of the swimming pool, and Nate did a cannonball over top of them. They screamed and splashed him when he emerged, spitting water everywhere. "Looks like everyone is having a good time," Grace said and tried not to sound sarcastic.

Brandon shrugged.

Grace wished that Jessica would go away, but she stood there with a slight smile on her face like she was enjoying being the third wheel. Except, Grace thought, it was *she* who was the intruder.

A flash of anger overtook her, and she said to Brandon in a measured voice, "Well, *you* must have been having a good time to not have found any time at all to check-in."

"You were the one who decided not to come earlier," he countered. His tone was cold, and Grace's anger was mixed with confusion. She *had* decided not to come earlier, but it hadn't been much of a choice. He had known that.

Alyssa appeared with two cups for Jessica and Brandon. "Oh, hey," she said, the only one who looked remotely pleased to see Grace. "You finally made it. How did the lunch go with your dad?"

Grace didn't answer Alyssa. She watched Brandon chug the contents of the cup while Jessica took a sip and gazed at Grace over the rim of her cup. Grace stood in front of them, her legs parted slightly and her back rigid. The hair stood up on the back of her neck, and while a part of her had been worried all day about Jessica getting her claws into Brandon, she hadn't thought it would happen.

It appeared that she'd been wrong.

Alyssa was clearly uncomfortable and torn between the need for Jessica's approval and her newer and untested friendship with Grace.

Grace didn't have time for Alyssa. She needed to quickly decide how to play this, and her decision would mean everything for her relationship with Brandon.

She had two choices. She could make a scene and yell, forcing his attention onto her and her anger or hurt. Or she could bury her hurt deep down and act like she didn't care. Act like Brandon meant less to her than he did.

In that split second, the faces of both her mother and her aunt flashed into her comprehension. In the end, she was more Mariah than Lucy, and she smiled placidly despite the churning in her chest.

"Far be it from me to interrupt your good time," she said as smoothly as she could manage and turned around before she registered any sort of reaction on the part of either Brandon or Jessica. She found an empty spot at the edge of a lounge chair to set down her cut while she freed herself of the tank top and the shorts that covered her skimpy bikini.

She noted the looks and murmurs of several other guys in attendance and made another quick decision. Nate was an idiot. Eli too timid and gentle. Some of the other boys she barely knew at all. But Tanner was a familiar face. Tanner's father was a state senator. And while Tanner wasn't as kind, smart, or athletic as Brandon, nor was he anywhere near as good-looking, he would do for tonight.

Grace walked over to where he stood with three other boys, grabbed his hand, and pulled him into the swimming pool.

"Well, okay," he said thickly, as she looked at him, willing herself not to glance toward the far end of the patio. "I thought you were with Brandon." His words were slightly slurred.

She tilted her head to one side. "Does it look like I'm with Brandon?"

It turned out she didn't have to look at all because Tanner did it for her. "I guess not with Jessica Reed's tongue down his throat."

Grace's heart lurched, but she kept her gaze steady. For once, she wished she had listened to her mother and had stayed home. If she and Brandon were going to break up, did she need to bear witness to the events that would lead to the inevitable?

She sank underwater, opening her eyes so that she could see the distorted bodies around her. She would be able to cry under here, and no one would even know, but the thing was, she didn't feel like crying. She just felt numb.

She came back up, and Tanner was looking at her with a lecherous gaze. It made her want to lurch away, but she still leaned into his slick body, aware that what she was doing wasn't right. Then again, neither was what Brandon was doing.

Grace also knew that Tanner was no angel. It's not as if he would have any notions that one night during a stupid party was going to lead anywhere anyway.

Besides, she could do worse than Tanner Harris. Her mother would probably have been happier with this choice than she was with Brandon.

Grace looked up into his face. His nose was too wide, his eyes too small, his mouth too thin, his teeth too big. But she kissed him.

# CHAPTER ELEVEN

G race forced herself not to gag, and she wasn't sure if she was gagging because she was disgusted with herself, disgusted with Brandon, or disgusted with Tanner. It could have been all three of those things.

When she pulled away from him, his hands were around her waist under the water and slowly inching further down the back slope of her hips. She reached behind herself, grabbed his hands, and held them in front of her.

She did not want that.

He gave her a lopsided and fuzzy smile. "Little bit of a tease, huh?" he said playfully.

She tried to smile back, but she just wanted to get out of the pool and out of that house. "Maybe we can just talk for a little bit," she said instead.

"What do you want to talk about?" he asked. He had trouble forming the question and didn't wait for an answer. He leaned his head closer, and she turned her head while she attempted to hold his hands in front of her.

"I don't know anything about you," she said. "Have

you looked at colleges yet?"

He managed to free one of her hands, and he used it to grab her nose, pinching it. It hurt, and Grace batted his hand away. He reached behind her again and pressed her up against him.

His eyes were glassy. He was drunk, but not drunk enough. "You're cute," he said, and she thought maybe she could keep him distracted.

Grace managed to pull away from him again. "My mom wants me to look at Ivy League schools, but I'm not sure that's something I want."

"You know what I want?" he growled. He grabbed her again, this time more roughly than she was expecting. She wasn't ready for it and had no leverage standing in the water.

He kissed her again, forcing his mouth on hers. She tried to pull back, but he was stronger than her. And she had started this. She felt a little bit panicked but figured she'd just ride this out until she could get away. She had her wits about her. She wasn't drunk, and she wasn't helpless. When he finally pulled away, she took advantage of the slackness in his arms and swam to the other side of the pool.

"Hey," he said, splashing after her. "Where are you going?" He no longer sounded like he was joking around. He sounded angry.

She may have had less to drink and swam faster, but the pool wasn't that big, and she felt like a goldfish being pursued by a piranha.

Now others had started to watch this game, and some of the girls looked on uncomfortably, but they didn't make eye contact with Grace.

She hoisted herself up and climbed out, looked around. Brandon and Jessica were nowhere to be found. Had they left together? Gone to a far-off corner? An empty bedroom? The split second of wondering had cost her time. And she may have miscalculated because as fast as she moved in the water, Tanner moved faster out of it. He was behind her in an instant, pushing his body against her back while he pinned her right arm against her body and circled her tight. "Come on," he said against her ear. "You want this."

Nate was cheering him on, but he had had too much to drink. She didn't think he had any idea what was happening. Eli looked uncomfortable, but a boy like Eli wasn't going to stop a boy like Tanner. There were other guys there, but they either weren't paying attention or were looking away.

Brandon wouldn't have let this happen, but Brandon wasn't around when she needed him.

Alyssa came up to them and gave Grace a concerned look. "Hey, Tanner," she said, touching his forearm. "You want to dance?"

Grace was aware of a song playing on the speakers through some hidden sound system.

Tanner ignored Alyssa and instead put his tongue

in Grace's ear. She found that she couldn't move at all. Her head was pinned against him, and her arms were useless. He was behind her, and there was nowhere to kick. Even if she managed to make contact and get free, she thought he would just chase her down. And there was no one here who was going to stop him.

Alyssa's voice was beside her but sounded faraway. Tanner swatted the other girl away like a pesky insect.

*This is my fault*, Grace thought and panicked. She had initiated this. When she struggled, Tanner held her tighter, squeezing her and restricting her breath.

The vodka had been a mistake. She could still feel the soft fuzziness penetrating her mind and her body. She was weakened, if not drunk.

Grace made eye contact with another girl in the pool. Lindsey, who was an acquaintance. Lindsey had the decency to look guilty as she glanced away, not sure what to do or say. This girl was not in their typical circle. She was probably happy just to have been invited to this party. She wasn't going to go out on a limb for a girl she barely knew.

Alyssa's voice was more urgent this time. "Hey, Tanner. Let her go." She could feel Alyssa tugging at Tanner's arms. It was enough of a distraction that his grip loosened, and Grace was able to free herself at least.

He spun around and tried to grab her again.

Alyssa grabbed his wrist. "Hey," she cooed. "Come

on."

Grace grabbed her clothes from the ground where she'd stupidly tossed them.

But Tanner wasn't put off that easily. "She wants it," he said gruffly.

Alyssa pushed a cup into Tanner's hands, trying to distract him.

Grace didn't bother to dress, just ran, carrying her clothes through the house, still dripping pool water on the smooth tiled floors. She fished around in the pocket of her shorts and gave a silent prayer of thanks that her key fob had not fallen out.

She had almost made it to the front door before she was lifted from behind. Tanner was carrying her up the stairs. Alyssa was nowhere to be found. No one else seemed to be close by. "Put me down," Grace screamed.

Her yelling did not seem to bother him in the least, and she scraped and scratched at his forearms, not caring at all if they both tumbled down the curved staircase. She kicked at empty air, attempted to kick behind her, but made no contact.

He squeezed her hard, and she thought he might break her ribs.

She started to cry, but it didn't matter. This was going to happen, and she was now stone sober, about to become a victim and a statistic.

He entered an empty room and threw her down

onto a bed.

With her limbs finally free, Grace kicked him hard in the thigh and scrabbled to the side of the bed.

Tanner grunted but easily grabbed her around her ankle and strongarmed her back into position. Then he slapped her hard across the face.

Temporarily stunned, she stared up at him, and something flashed across his face—a recognition of impropriety. It gave her a split second of hope.

But then his face morphed into something else entirely—an animal look, feral and mean. He ripped off the inconsequential fabric of her bathing suit, and once that barrier was gone, she had nothing left. She shut her eyes and drifted away because what else was there for her to do? This was her fault.

☦ ☦ ☦

Grace opened her eyes and looked around Lucy's cottage. It was silent. *She* was silent.

Lucy was in the chair across from her exactly where Logi had been earlier. Her aunt was watching her closely.

Grace looked around, half expecting to see someone else in the room, though she had no idea who that might have been.

Unlike her other dreams that had faded quickly and seemed scrambled and confused, she remembered this one. She remembered every detail of what had been happening to her in that other world.

"Okay?" Lucy asked, and Grace wasn't sure if Lucy was asking if she was okay or if the situation was understood.

"I'm not sure," Grace said. She sat up, felt no pain in her body. Again, she felt numb.

"Things happen to us all," Lucy said. "Sometimes they define us, and sometimes we define them. But whether we accept them or fight them, they change us in one way or another."

"Is that why I'm here?" Grace asked. "Because I was defined?"

"The story isn't over."

"Do I get to choose how it ends?"

"You always get to choose your ending, but it may not be what you expected. We often surprise ourselves."

Grace wasn't ready to think about this latest revelation in her life because she knew there would be more. Despite the terrible thing that had happened to her in another reality, she knew it was not over. And she suspected the rest of it was much, much worse.

Grace also knew that what had happened to her was not the only reason she was here. There was some intersection with her mother and the woman across from her. There was some lesson that she needed to learn for all of them. And that included these souls with whom she was interacting in this other world.

To Lucy, she said, "Tell me about Jon."

Lucy tipped her head back against the cushion of the chair, and Grace could tell she was thinking about some boy of long ago, not the man who had been here just a few hours ago. How many lives did one soul possess?

"Jon was in love with your mother," Lucy said wistfully. "I wish you could have seen her back then— completely sure of what she wanted to do with her life. We had no money. She wore my hand-me-downs, and we mostly ate out of our garden, but it was as if she knew she had a destiny beyond this simple life. For him, living with his grandparents in a similarly run-down existence, it was impossible not to be attracted by her overwhelming belief in a life outside of this one. I didn't understand her. And I was jealous. I wanted to be that impossibly confident in my beliefs. Henry was bewitched by her, as was Jon."

"Were you in love with him then too?"

Lucy shook her head. "Not at first. He was just the boy down the street."

"And did you have your own plans?"

"I felt like I needed to stay and help your grandmother and Henry. University wasn't my destiny. *This* was my destiny." She smiled, then she held up a finger. "Just to be clear, I didn't want the things that Mariah wanted. I didn't envy her wandering spirit, just her overwhelming spirit. I envied who she was."

"But not who she is now?"

Lucy shook her head, then seemed to choose her words carefully. "When you're young, you can be fierce in your beliefs. Before life makes you timid."

Grace would not have described her mother as timid, but she supposed the things that had happened to her had changed her. The failed marriage, the career that was good but probably not quite as glamorous or as lucrative as she'd expected it to be. There was a lot of political pressure and baggage that came with what Mariah did for a living. Grace knew that she was often exhausted from more than just the long hours.

"And how did Jon fit into her life back then?" Grace asked, moving backward.

"If Mariah was the wind, Jon was a tree. He was rooted, solid, and with as much strength as she may have tried to push against him, he wasn't moving."

"She tried to get him to move?"

Lucy shrugged. "He never said, and neither did she. But he adored her, and she adored him. I believe she probably thought she could have gotten him to change for her."

Grace was quiet, and so was Lucy. There were many more questions that Grace wanted to ask, not only about her mother but about Lucy. And about herself. Because she had realized that she wasn't in this spot by accident, nor was she entirely sure that she was ever going to be able to leave.

What she had thought were dreams were—she was sure—glimpses of another reality, and she didn't think that they had happened in the past. It was almost as if she were living two realities at one time. As if time were bubbling up in parallel existences. In one of those realities, she was still alive...

She touched her leg, and the flesh was solid. She could feel this fabric on her skin. She could smell the sweet mildew smell of the interior of the cabin. She could hear the breeze in the trees, the sound of the birds, the rush of the rapids in the distance.

Lucy said, "The veil between this life and the next is much thinner than we could imagine."

Grace didn't know if Lucy had read her thoughts, but she stood from the sofa, needing to be alone just then. She walked outside, down the rickety stairs, and when she reached the end of the lane, she looked back at the cabin. It appeared much like the day that her mother had left her here, except Grace thought she could detect the aura of life around the building that had not been there at first.

She turned and continued to the river bank, which was rushing at a swift pace from some unknown place or time. Grace sat down. She had many questions but few answers. Asking Lucy was like peeling back the carefully laid veneer of what she'd thought was a perfectly ordinary life. She didn't want to see the blood and veins beneath. She didn't want to know the pain and the tears that had laid the groundwork for something that had turned out to be precious and fragile. She wanted to hold on to the illusion for just a little while longer.

She wasn't sure how long she had been sitting there along, throwing small stones into the rush of water and watching them disappear beneath the surface.

She heard them before she saw them—the two little girls, Sophie and Anna. They came as quietly as you would expect two little girls of their age to make their way through leaves and limbs. The two kittens followed along like small dogs.

They didn't seem surprised to see her, nor did they seem pleased. She simply was, as she sat on a log by the edge of the river.

"Hello," she said.

They stood on either side of her and looked out at the river.

"We came to keep you company," said Sophie.

Grace looked around for Jon. She knew that he would not be far away.

Both kittens were pouncing on the blanket of dried leaves and twigs.

"How are Rosemary and Lily?" Grace asked.

"Brandon," Sophie corrected.

"Brandon," Grace repeated, and her throat closed. She remembered Brandon standing with Jessica. And she remembered what came after, at least to a point.

She would not explore that now.

Anna, the elf, leaned her small solid body against Grace while picking the petals off of a daisy. "He loves me… He loves me not," she said under her breath.

Grace watched her, and Sophie watched Grace. "Mommy taught us that," she said helpfully.

"Is your mommy at home?"

"Yes," Anna answered. "She's in her new home."

Grace didn't ask any questions. She felt as if the ground was shifting beneath her feet. One minute the earth was there, and the next, she found herself floating with no foundation.

She had suspicions about her own experience… But she wasn't quite ready to face those suspicions.

Sophie was still watching with her omniscient hazel eyes.

"My mom is at home, too," Grace said, drawing the parallel between her experience and that of these children.

"Does she miss you?" Anna asked.

Grace remembered the tires crunching on the driveway, the cloud of dust on the dry earth. She shook her head at Sophie, her smile sad. "At first, I thought she wanted me to leave, but the longer I'm here, the more that I think she probably misses me."

Anna picked up another flower. "Will you go back now?"

"I'm not sure if I can."

"Daddy told us that we can't go back yet."

Some of the hope drained from Grace's heart.

"We have to wait here for Mommy," said Anna, unconcerned.

"Maybe I have to do the same thing," Grace murmured.

Anna laughed suddenly and dropped her flower. Brandon had bounded a few feet away, chasing a small white butterfly. "Brandon, what are you doing," she yelled with glee, joining in the game and trying to capture the flitting white creature herself.

Grace smiled but was keenly aware of Sophie's gaze.

"What happened?" Grace asked, not sure if Sophie would answer her or even understand the question.

She should have known better. "There was a fire. Mommy made it out with me, but they couldn't find Anna. Daddy went back in for her, and I ran back in too."

Grace shut her eyes, couldn't imagine the pain that their mother had experienced. To have had at least her husband and one of her children safe, and then to have none of them...

"Why did you run back in?" Grace asked.

She looked over at Anna. "I couldn't let her go without me."

"But what about your mom?"

Sophie turned her gaze back to Grace. "It's only a few minutes."

# CHAPTER TWELVE

G race walked from the river to the house slowly. She left the girls there to play with the butterflies and the kittens, where she could see them through the trees. When she started back up the driveway, she noticed that Jon was leaning over the front porch steps and was wearing a tool pouch around his waist.

Such an ordinary thing—fixing those dilapidated steps. Was that necessary in this existence?

"Those little ones bothering you?" he asked and watched him test the wood with one foot, then lean over to test the others with his hands. She realized that this man would be fixing things in any existence. It had much less to do with her experience than it had with his.

"I noticed that these could use a few nails when we were here earlier. Thought I'd do Lucy a favor and fix them for her."

"That's nice of you."

"It's the neighborly thing to do."

Grace was quiet.

"Something on your mind?" he asked. It was an

invitation, and she walked inside.

"I believe I know why I'm here. I'm just trying to figure out what it is that I need to learn."

"The things that you need to learn will come to you." He crouched down and carefully lifted an old board from its place on the second step. Then he turned it over and nailed it back into place. "This will do until I can get some better wood."

"I'd like to ask you about my mother," Grace said.

Jon finished pounding in the nail and then turned around and sat on the step. "I thought you might."

"You said that you were in love with her."

"I was," he said simply. "The love of my young life."

"What about your wife?"

He didn't seem surprised by her question or her knowledge. "The love of my adult life. You can have more than one love, you know. The trouble comes with you listen to…" He waved his hand in the air and continued, "…whoever it is that seems to have made up the rules of love. There's not always just one person that you need to spend the rest of your life with. Doesn't always work that way." He looked at her levelly. "Does it?"

She averted her eyes.

"Did you come back here for Lucy after the fire?"

"I came back here because it was home, and I wanted the girls to know this place. This place is part of my soul."

Lucy had said something similar.

"And Mariah had grown up here, and Lucy was here. I suppose I needed to make peace with all of that, too."

"And did you?"

"Getting there," he said. "You look like your mom, you know. When she was young. The eyes. That determination in your chin."

Grace shook her head. "She always knew what she wanted."

"You sure about that?"

She kicked at a large stone that had been embedded in the earth. She wondered how long it had been there. If her mother or her aunt had kicked the same stone when they'd been young.

"Did you keep in touch with her after she'd left for college?"

"For a while. She'd made it clear that it was over between us if I wouldn't move with her. But she didn't want to completely let go either."

"When did you start dating Lucy?"

He hung his head and stared at his hands interlaced between his knees. "It wasn't a conscious decision. I didn't decide to date Lucy because I couldn't have Mariah. She was here, and I was here. We were friends. Henry had been injured on the railroad. She was helping her mother, and I was helping them with chores around the house. It was a natural progression from friends to… more."

"But it wasn't love."

"It was new, and sweet, and easy. Lucy is a soft glow, where Mariah is a stiff wind. It didn't have time to grow into love. And I don't know if it ever would have. But we never got the chance to find out."

"What happened?"

"I can't speak for Mariah or for Lucy. I can only tell my story."

Grace nodded. That's all she was asking.

"After a few months away at school, Mariah came home unexpectedly. I never found out the real reason she was there. Mariah was never one for surprises. Henry's health had started to deteriorate, and your grandmother was upstairs with him. Mariah found Lucy and me in the kitchen. We weren't doing anything, really. I think I had my arms around her."

He stopped talking and tilted his head back, looking toward the sky.

"Neither of you told her that you'd started to date?"

"Like I said, it was new. I don't think we wanted to make something out of it if it weren't going to last. At least, that's what I'd told myself."

She waited until he'd processed those emotions and continued. "Mariah was extremely upset. She yelled that we'd both betrayed her, accused us of all sorts of things, told us that we were dead to her. Neither of us could break through her tirade, and of course, your grandmother had heard the commotion and was trying to make peace. Mariah turned her back on her mother, too. Looking back, it was probably understandable. Afterward, I thought that she had probably come home because she wanted to try to make it work, even if it had to be long-distance."

He stopped, and Grace said, "But that's not the end of the story."

He shook his head. "The rest is not my story to tell."

She knew that it was Lucy's.

"And then you'd decided to leave this place for good?"

He shrugged, picked up his hammer, and passed it from one had to the other. "I moved away shortly after that day. There wasn't anything for me here anymore. Met Rose while I was working a construction job up north. We married quickly and had the girls shortly after that. She knew all about Mariah and Lucy and understood why I needed to get away from here, from the memories. The fire was an accident—a short in a wire in the middle of the night. We all should have gotten out, but Anna wasn't in her bed. Little elf had a habit of sleepwalking and was in the family room. I went back in, and Sophie ran in after me. Rose would have run in too, but a neighbor held her back."

"Is she okay?"

"She's strong, and I talk to her all the time. She talks back."

"Sophie told me that she'd only be waiting for a minute."

He laughed. "Sophie knows a lot that the rest of us don't know, which is why she ran back in after me. Somehow, she knew we'd all be together and that her mother would be fine. I don't know." He stood. "But Sophie does."

Lucy came out of the house then. "Oh, I didn't know you were here," she said, smiling at Jon. "Where are the girls?"

They came bounding up the driveway then, flying with their arms out to their sides.

Lucy yelled, "Come on in. I made a pie!"

The girls flashed by and into the house in a blur.

Grace had trouble believing that this wasn't the land of the living. She supposed it was just a different sort of living.

Jon had his hand on the door handle when Grace asked suddenly, "When was the fire?"

"October 17, 2008."

He walked into the house, but Grace stood utterly still as two things hit her. Sophie should be the same age as she was right now. And that was the date that her dad had moved out. She didn't think that was a coincidence.

✝ ✝ ✝

Jon and the girls didn't stay long that afternoon. He tousled Grace's hair on the way out, and it occurred to her that under different circumstances, this man may have been her father.

Would Grace have known a sister? Would she have ended up rushing back into a burning house?

Lucy was wrapping up the pie when Grace walked into the kitchen. "Jon said that you'd asked him some questions," Lucy said.

"I thought I had a right to know."

"All of our stories are connected."

"Which is why I'm here."

Lucy nodded.

"Jon told me about my mom coming home unexpectedly."

"I used to think about that night and how things could have been different. If she had called. If she had walked in thirty seconds earlier or thirty seconds later. If I had gone upstairs, instead of your grandmother, to check on Henry."

"You think that she was coming home to try to make things work with him?"

Lucy turned toward Grace. "I know that's why she was here. And he would have gone back to her. But none of that matters now."

But it did matter. It mattered to Grace, and she was

certain that it would matter to her mother. She said those words to Lucy, who shook her head. "You can't go back."

"But you can change your actions moving forward if you have the truth."

"There's more than one version of the truth."

"Maybe your sister needs to hear yours."

Lucy opened her mouth to say something, then shut it again. "Not all of you is like your mother, you know." She flicked a dishtowel against the counter. She was quiet for so long that Grace didn't think she was going to speak again.

"Henry had asked for water," Lucy said, "and your grandmother had taken it to him." She touched the edge of the sink. "We were standing right here." Then she reached out her hand as if a younger version of herself were there at that very moment. Grace watched as Lucy became someone else in front of her. She watched as a younger version of Jon appeared, standing close, but not uncomfortably so. Grace knew that the veil between time had been lifted again, in this reality. And she was an observer, not a participant.

The younger Lucy looked a lot like she did now. Long blond hair, round cheeks, and full mouth. She was pretty, but not beautiful. Kindness radiated from her, and an internal comfort that she couldn't ever imagine coming from the prickly Mariah.

The younger version of Lucy said, "He doesn't have

much time left," and a tear escaped from the corner of her eye. Grace knew that she was talking about Henry, her grandfather, who was dying somewhere upstairs.

Languid and lean, Jon slowly, shyly wrapped his arms around Lucy's waist. It was not romantic or sensual, though it was intimate, as witnessing someone else's grief often was.

Grace sensed another entity entering the room, and she turned.

There was no question that it was her mother in the doorway beside her: the wavy auburn mane, the sharp green eyes, the stormy energy. But there was a presence to this being that didn't belong to her mother, who moved at a pace meant to force time into trying to keep up with her.

Lucy and Jon didn't notice at first, but Grace saw this young woman's face wearing a thousand emotions in the space of a second—from pure joy to utter devastation.

Grace's heart broke.

Jon noticed her first. "Mariah," he said, pulling away from Lucy as if he'd been burned.

Lucy did not seem to register the damage that had just occurred, and she smiled radiantly at her younger sister, moving toward her as if to embrace her.

Mariah took two full steps back and said, "How could you?" It was all directed at Lucy.

A look of confusion crossed Lucy's face before she

glanced at Jon. "Oh, Riah," she said, using a derivative that Grace had never heard. "It's not—Please let me explain."

"I don't think you need to explain anything to me. I can see quite well what's going on."

Jon stepped forward, animated. "Mariah, you need to understand—"

"*I* need to understand?" she yelled. "No, I think *you* need to understand what this," she waved her hand between the two of them, "what *this* means."

An older woman appeared, and Grace realized that this was her grandmother. "Mariah," she tried to break in but was immediately cut off.

"You knew about this and didn't tell me?" Mariah demanded of her mother.

"If you'd just let us explain—" Jon tried.

"I don't want to hear anything from you!"

"You left," Lucy managed to break in. Her voice was quiet by intense. "You left us all here and went off to do your own thing even though dad is upstairs dying. Even though Jon asked you not to go. You went anyway. And you can't have it both ways."

Mariah came close to Lucy's face. "And you've been waiting for that, haven't you? Waiting for me to leave so that you could have this life all to yourself." Her face was red, and while there were no tears, it looked as if she were about to burst at any moment.

Lucy kept her composure. "I'm not going to apologize for your misunderstanding, nor will I make changes based on your jealousy. You've always been selfish."

"I'm selfish," Mariah spat a mean laugh. "That's hilarious. When as soon as my back is turned, you steal my boyfriend."

"I'm not your boyfriend," Jon said. "You made that very clear."

Another movement caught Grace's eye, and she noticed Henry in the doorway. But this Henry was bandaged and pale. The face may have been smoother, but there was less life in this version of her grandfather than the man with whom she had gone fishing a few days earlier.

Mariah turned on Jon. "This is what you've been waiting for, too?"

"Of course not. I loved you," he yelled, "And you told me to go. Did you want me to wait for you forever?"

She waited a beat too long to answer. Then she said, "Of course not. But I didn't expect you to go after my sister."

"It wasn't like that," Lucy said.

"Why don't you tell me what it was like, then," Mariah challenged.

"Okay, let's all just calm down," her grandmother said. No one had noticed Henry standing sadly in the shadow of the doorway.

Mariah slashed the air with her hand. "I will not be calm. I came back—" She stopped herself quickly, and a sob bubbled up. She quickly swallowed it down and stared levelly at Lucy, ignoring everyone else in the room. "You are dead to me," she said calmly, definitively.

"Mariah," her grandmother said. But Mariah held up a hand and continued to look at Lucy, who had dimmed. "What you've done has altered the course of my life," she said. "Do what you will. Marry Jon, have babies with Jon. I will never speak to you again, look at you again, utter your name again. You have erased yourself from my existence."

Henry came through the door then, and Grace thought that Mariah might take it all back, but she just said, "I'm sorry, Dad," and walked back out the way she came.

Grace heard the sound of a car and the crunch of tires, exactly the sound she had heard when her mother had left her here.

As if frozen in time, no one moved, until Lucy ran to the front door, and the low rumble of what could have only been Henry's truck sounded in the driveway.

The vision faded away then, and Lucy was standing alone at the sink. The color had not yet returned to her cheeks.

"I went after her," Lucy said. "But it was raining, and the roads were unfamiliar. At the time, there were no phones or GPS. I was trying to drive on memory. I don't remember exactly what happened, but I crossed over the line on a divided highway and ended up hitting a tractor-trailer truck head-on."

Grace was quiet for a moment. "Why did she say you'd killed yourself?"

"I think part of her believed that I had. I think part of *me* believed I had." She took a breath.

"And now you're here."

"I've never really left."

"And Jon came back too. Sophie said that they're waiting for their mom."

"It's not a bad place to wait and rest." She touched Grace's cheek.

They were both quiet for a long time, lost in their own thoughts and memories.

Lucy finally said, softly, "But you've got some unfinished business waiting for you."

"I don't want to go back," Grace said. She couldn't go back. Couldn't play out the rest of that horrible scene. Couldn't face what she suspected was going to happen after.

Lucy smiled. "We live life forward but understand it backward. Go," she said. "Live. There will be time to understand later."

# CHAPTER THIRTEEN

The heaviness of a solid body pressed against Grace's torso and neck. She couldn't turn her head, and her wrists were pinned to the side. She opened her eyes and focused on the slat in a Venetian blind that covered the window to her right, refusing to allow any other thoughts to enter her mind. She breathed into the darkness outside.

She could feel him moving.

She saw Lucy's face floating in front of her, and she willed herself back to the cabin in the woods. Back to Henry, Jon, Sophie, and Anna. And she could almost get herself there, she thought. The earthy smell of the river was in her nose.

Then, with a sudden movement, the body was gone, ripped away. She was completely exposed on the bed. Cold, her hair still damp, her body hot.

It took her a few seconds to process what was happening, but then, in slow motion, she saw Brandon cock his fist and punch a recovering Tanner in his face. Tanner was still impaired. His swimming trunks impeded his movement, and he was unable to react. He stumbled back, almost falling onto Grace.

She rolled away, spotted a decorative blanket on a rocking chair in the corner of the room, and grabbed it, holding it up over her naked body.

She watched in horror as Tanner righted himself and lunged toward Brandon, who appeared to be completely sober. Brandon hit him again, harder, and Tanner went down.

Grace stared at the slack face of her attacker.

She felt absolutely nothing. No anger, no fear, no disgust. She felt like she was outside herself watching all this happen to a girl who was familiar to her but was not her.

Grace felt Brandon's gaze on her, and she looked at him. There was a part of her who wanted to fall into his arms and pretend this night had never happened. But she saw what she perceived as an accusation in his eyes.

Then Jessica was in the doorway, lobbing a smirk at Grace—a half-smile that seemed to say, "I know what you did. I know it backfired. You've been humiliated, and I got the guy."

Without one word having been exchanged, Grace ran from the room.

Her shorts were on the stairs, where she must have dropped them. She swept them up, again saying a silent prayer to the universe that the fob was still in the shallow pocket.

An audience had formed at the bottom of the stairs,

attracted by the yelling or the scent of a fight. They certainly hadn't been interested in helping her when she'd needed it. Now, naked and barely covered by a small blanket, she rushed past them. No one stopped her, and she didn't wait to see if anyone was laughing or snickering in her direction. These were not her friends.

Outside, she fled barefoot to her car. Before she could get in, she leaned over and emptied the scant contents of her stomach onto the lawn.

A voice yelled, "Hey," and she turned her head to see the neighbor heading toward her—the one with whom she'd made eye contact earlier.

"Are you okay?" he yelled. "Do you need help?"

She fumbled with the button on the key fob and then pulled the door open.

"You can't drive," she heard him exclaim, but she got the car started and backed up without looking behind her. She sideswiped the car parked to her right, which hadn't been there when she'd pulled into the party earlier, but she didn't stop. She drove out of the driveway without looking for traffic on the residential street.

She pulled out onto the highway, and another wave of nausea hit, the reality of what had just happened hitting her hard. She seemed to be floating in the images of the evening—Jessica leaning into Brandon's chest, the feeling of Tanner's slick body under her hands, the push of his tongue into her mouth, the smell of his skin as he picked her up from behind, the taste of his sweat while he pushed himself against her.

Her head pounded, and she whimpered. The lights from the oncoming traffic seemed to come directly at her, and she broke out into a cold sweat. As she swerved into the right lane, a car came up fast on the driver's side. The driver began to lay on the car's horn, and she glanced over. She thought it was Brandon, but she couldn't tell. The world was underwater. Or she was in a fishbowl.

The driver had the window down and mouthed something at her. She squinted, trying to make out the features, the words coming out of the open mouth. She fumbled for the window release, looked down, slamming on the breaks. Another horn blared, and she swerved again. When she looked back up, the car was no longer beside her. Her window was down, however, and the wind blew into her face. Still naked, except for the blanket that was half draped across her body, she shivered violently.

And then the car was beside her again, and, as if the air had knocked some of the reality back into her, she saw that it was Brandon. Through the wind, she could hear him yelling, "Pull over."

She wanted to believe that he'd come after her because he cared about her, but she knew that wasn't the case. She stared straight ahead, both hands gripping the steering wheel.

He yelled something else, the wind and noise of the

traffic distorting the sound of his voice and words.

She heard as clear as if they'd been spoken in her ear, "Grace, I love you!"

Her mouth open, she looked back at him. She wanted to tell him that she loved him too, that she was sorry for everything, that they could get past anything.

He smiled, and she smiled back.

And then, a violent explosion of metal as Brandon was yanked away. Her head swiveled, and she thought she screamed before the bright white crack, the explosion of light, and the shattering of her reality into diamond splinters of past, present, and future.

✝ ✝ ✝

Her eyes flew open, and she sat straight up in the twin bed. The sunlight was streaming through the windows, and a soft breeze cooled the air. There was light here, where she had come from darkness.

Her skin was damp with sweat, and she shivered slightly.

She glanced down at the clothes that she had been wearing early in the day.

Was that right? Had she just taken a short nap?

As she came back into herself, the dream/memory arranged itself into Grace's awareness, coming to damp and uncomfortable life.

The headache, the party, the swimming pool. Jessi-

ca and Brandon. The scene in the bedroom. The bright
white light of the shattered night.

She groaned, flopped back, and rolled over onto
her stomach, staring at the tiny pink flowers. It seemed
impossible that she had woken up here, back in this
bed. In this alternate reality.

She forced herself up and into the tiny bathroom.
She splashed water onto her face from the lukewarm
stream of water out of the tap.

She remembered the swimming pool, the cool
water over her bare skin, the feeling of that boy's hands
on her.

She dried her face on the rough towel and stared at
her face into the mirror. Bare of makeup and pretenses,
she looked to herself to be much younger than she was.
There were no more dark shadows under her eyes here;
just a level gaze that held more understanding than she
wished she had.

She walked down the narrow staircase, past the
peeling paint and rusty nails. She touched the nails
with the tip of her fingers as she walked. Had they once
held photos? Awkwardly posed senior portraits of her
mother and Lucy?

Grace knew that her mother had a bunch of old
photographs in the closet in her bedroom. Grace didn't
think she'd been explicitly forbidden from looking at
them, but she'd never been invited to explore them
either. She should have been more curious about her
mother's life than she had been.

She saw the profile of Lucy on the front porch on the rickety-looking rocking chair. In real life, she didn't think that old rocking chair would have held a person. But this wasn't real life.

On the other hand, the place from which she had just returned in her mind seemed much more like the dream as she looked around this very real house in this tactile experience.

She stepped out on the front porch, and Logi, who was nestled in Lucy's lap, squinted up at her sleepily, always watching.

Grace sat down on the porch floor, leaning her back against a railing that seemed precarious even in this existence.

Lucy looked at her. And Grace didn't know what she expected. Words of wisdom, maybe. Some treatise on the illusory nature of life or the impermanence of any existence.

"It'll take some time to process," Lucy said, and Grace didn't tell her that she hadn't even allowed herself to explore the memory. But maybe that's why she was here. To reflect and remember at her own pace, on her own time.

"You can stay here as long as you'd like."

"Where else would I go?"

Lucy didn't answer.

"In life, we aren't given the luxury of precognition," Lucy said calmly. "Only hindsight. And hindsight does us no good if used incorrectly."

"But I've messed everything up," Grace responded. She allowed herself just a glimpse back at the memory. She couldn't quite yet call it what it was. She shifted on the floor of the porch, leaning her head to look out at the trees. A gray squirrel perched on his hind legs, nibbling at an acorn, then ran up a tree with its frantic movements, spiraling around to an unknown destination.

"Humans tend to do that," Lucy said, smiling. "*Look at what I've done.*"

"And my mother," Grace said, because she knew that her mother was just as at fault for Lucy's situation as Lucy herself was.

"There is no blame," said Lucy. "No regret. Just now."

"But you can't learn without looking back," argued Grace.

Logi came to Grace. He purred and wound around her legs, bent at the knee.

"And you *do* look back. You look back, and you learn. And then you move forward with what you've got."

"Even here?"

"Especially here."

"But I can't stay here forever."

"Of course not. No one stays anywhere forever."

"You and Henry did."

"Oh, no, Gracie. This is not our forever."

Grace frowned and looked up at the house. The

garden was tended, and the kitchen was stocked. The books were on the shelves. They didn't just appear there by themselves.

"This is where we've come to wait for you."

† † †

The sun had started to sink in the sky, and Grace found herself restless and confused. Alone. What exactly was she supposed to do with her time here? And where would she go next?

She had thoroughly examined the events of the last day in her life as she wandered in the forest. She thought about the assault and her role in it. She'd considered the defense of Brandon and subsequent horrific experience on that busy two-lane highway when she'd had no business driving at all.

She imagined that her mother had been informed of the events of that evening. Of Grace's condition. And Brandon's.

Now she was sitting by the bank of a small stream that led to the larger river, holding a small stick into the rush of water. The water bent around that stick, which was no obstacle at all, though it stood tall and solid in its path.

A golden glow glinted through the trees, and the light was visible, almost liquid rays as it illuminated the forest around her. She paused in her reverie to concentrate on this beauty. That was something that she had done enough of here, she knew. She wanted to hold the beauty in her hands, to reach out and—not to clutch it—rather caress it and allow it climb into her palms, gently. As if she were luring it there to land, like the lite of a butterfly.

She breathed it in and out, or something breathed her. She hardly knew anymore.

She had questions, of course. If she had perished in an accident, how was she here in this earthly existence, looking and breathing much like the girl who had been left behind? Was death just the other side of life, where you went to think about your mistakes?

Grace felt battered and bruised. She felt pushed and pulled and outside of her control. She had let go without meaning to.

She looked back at the stream, its water icy and clear, wending its way through the smooth rocks. She imagined the millions of microorganisms within that creek bed, teeming with some kind of life—earthly life or otherworldly life. And she thought that Death wasn't as much a goodbye as it was a shift in perception to a familiar place. And all of those worries that she'd held in her young heart hadn't been worth a millisecond of her time.

She'd felt, too, like she'd come back to life. That feeling she had after having been sick for a few days—lying under the blankets in the dim light and watching some mindless rerun of an inconsequential sitcom on the television. And then, the third day, she would emerge from her cocoon, and the sun shone on her face, the breeze caressing her face in welcome. "There you are, Grace," it said, and she breathed a hello from a place of joy in her heart that welcomed back the living world.

This is what she felt like now beside the creek bed.

She let go of her stick, watched it carried away quickly by the powerful flow toward the river. Its solidness was no match for the flow of the water. She crouched there on the balls of her feet, determined not to rise until she couldn't see her stick anymore. And then it was gone as if it had never been at all. As if she'd never held it in her hand. But maybe to the stick, she'd never existed either.

She stood then, and the light slanting through the forest was deeper and more golden, given depth by shadows and darkness.

A trick of the light exposed a man-shaped shadow in the distance, and Grace blinked, expecting it to disappear.

Instead of dissolving, it came closer, and she realized that a person was bearing down from the blank space behind the forest. It came closer, a silhouette, illuminated from behind. And then he emerged, smiling down on her.

She, exhilarated, enchanted, breathed, "Brandon."

# CHAPTER FOURTEEN

G race was in his arms, solid and real, and she cried
actual tears against his shoulder. She did not say,
"I thought I'd never see you again," because she
thought that he might disappear if the words left her
mouth. She knew that this was a gift.

He let her cry for a moment, and then he very gently placed his hands on her shoulders and guided her
away so that he could look at her. Or she could look at
him.

"It's good to see you," he said, and she nodded, not
quite able to speak yet.

He was handsome, with that one shock of hair that
tended to flop onto his forehead. His kind brown eyes.
His wide, gentle mouth. He was wearing a pair of well-
worn jeans and a red t-shirt that she had seen before.

He asked if she was okay, and she nodded again.
"I've been resting here," she managed to utter.

"This is a good place to rest," he answered, looking
around at the deepening shadows. But the sun
persisted from the other side of the trees.

"I know why you've come," she said, and he held

her hands in his. "I'm sorry," she whispered.

"My Grace," he said, holding her close again. "You have nothing to be sorry for. We are part of the ebb and flow of this existence. Our souls got to know each other for a time in the same existence. I'm really happy about that."

She started to cry again. "I'm happy about that, too," she sobbed, and he laughed, nudging her face up with his finger.

"This is not goodbye," he said. "I am in your heart, and you are in mine. You are a part of me, and I am a part of you."

It was one of those things that you said when you knew that you would never see the other person again, Grace knew, and while she resented it, she also believed it. Brandon was in her heart, and she would hold him close always.

They stood together for what seemed like an eternity. She guarded each second closely, sure that every passing moment would be the last.

"I don't have to go yet," he said. "Show me your cabin."

"How do you know it's a cabin?" she asked.

"I know a lot of things. Not sure how I know them."

They held hands as they walked, and as the light of the day faded for good, a silver full moon revealed itself just over the tops of the trees. The breeze made the forest restless, and the rush of the river was their music. At that moment, hand-in-hand in the forest, they had nothing to do but just be. There were no pretenses, no reasons to hurry or slow down, no need for dominance, improvement, or influence. They were completely and utterly free to just exist in this particular space-time continuum.

And still, Grace envied the seconds that could have been hours, days, months, years.

The irony was that they'd been free to do all this before. She didn't remember one time that they had just walked hand in hand without having someplace to be or an urgent need to get somewhere else. They had somehow, not so much missed their chance, as hadn't recognized that it was a chance at all. The number of other things to think about and do had gotten in the way.

They entered the darkened cabin, and Grace switched on a lamp, which gave a wan and comforting glow in the living room. No other sounds were present in the cabin, no other life but their own.

Brandon looked around. "This is a little different than your house."

She followed his gaze. "I think I like this better."

"I think I do too."

Now that there was so much to say, she found that she didn't know what to say at all. She felt awkward and clumsy. She felt like she needed to make a lasting impression. "I know you won't stay long," she said. "I wanted to ask you about that last night."

He sat down on the sofa, and she sat beside him.

"Why did you ignore me when I came to the house?"

He shut his eyes. "I wish there were an easy answer for that. Jessica had been telling me all day that you weren't the right girl for me. Dropping hints about how you weren't as sophisticated as the rest of the group." His words trailed off. "She said a lot of things that weren't true and that I knew I shouldn't be listening to. Things about you and your mother."

"My mother?"

He nodded. "She knew that your mother had grown up here." He looked around. "And that it was much more modest than what we were used to."

Grace frowned. She supposed it didn't matter, but how had the others known, when she had never thought to ask? She hardly saw how that mattered, even now.

"I didn't really care, Grace, but she was relentless, and then I didn't hear from you for most of the day. I know that I should have checked in on you. You were upset about your test, and you weren't feeling well. I knew that you'd seen your dad and would have been upset about that."

She nodded. "I was all of those things."

He shrugged. "I was just being selfish. At that moment, I just wanted something that wasn't complicated or serious. And Jessica was two-faced and petty, but what she wasn't was complicated or serious. She didn't make me think about my feelings or question my plans for the future." He shook his head. "It was stupid."

"I understand," she said because she did. How many times had she thought about the lack of complications at the cabin and been glad for it? There was something to be said for simplicity.

"And then you came in, looking tired and innocent. All I wanted to do was go somewhere quiet and talk to you. I got angry with myself for it. I wanted to be like those guys—like Tanner and Nate—for whatever reason. I wanted to have fun and drink and not think. I couldn't do that with you."

He stopped for a minute, and she was quiet too. She knew that none of this mattered anymore, but she still wanted to hear it.

"When I saw you with Tanner in that pool, I nearly lost my mind," he continued. "But I let Jessica pull me away. I shouldn't have done that. I should have stayed and gotten that creep off of you when I had the chance."

"I knew what I was doing," she said.

"See, but you didn't. You didn't know how he was going to react. Or how you were going to react."

"I should have, though. I was old enough to know better." He started to say something, and she shook her head. "How did you know to come and get me?"

"I heard you saying my name."

She furrowed her brow. "I couldn't say anything. He had my head pinned down."

"Then I knew you needed me. I could hear you needing me."

They were silent for a long time, pondering the mystery of the connection between two souls. Often no words or contact was needed. Grace had not appreciated those connections nearly enough. She was too caught up in the everchanging nature of time, trying to latch onto details that hadn't mattered in the first place without appreciating the sheer awesomeness of the experience itself. But she knew the experience itself, though made up of little moments, was too big to comprehend unless you were outside of it. Unless you were in a place like the one where she was now, where she could look back and be grateful.

She said, "If I hadn't run out, we wouldn't be where we are now." The events of that night played out in her memory. "I saw the crash."

"And our lives shattered into a million pieces," he said. Then he continued, "It was never going to last forever."

"It should have lasted longer."

"Who are we to know that? Besides, I'm all back together again.

"I don't feel back together," said Grace, feeling very

tired. But Brandon didn't look tired at all. He looked like Lucy and Jon and Henry. He looked at peace.

He smiled at her. "Ah, Grace," he said. "There's more work for you to do."

The light of the moon had slanted into the kitchen window, and she didn't know how much more self-reflection she could possibly do here.

"Not here," he said, "at home."

She stared at him. "I can't go back."

"Why not?"

She hesitated. "Because... The accident. Right?" She wasn't sure what she was asking. *Didn't I die?* **It** seemed like something that shouldn't need to be asked at all.

He said to her, "You can stay here as long as you want, but life will wait."

She wilted. The thought of facing all the damage she'd left behind and facing it without Brandon. She put her hands to her face.

"Hey," he said, gently pulling her hands from her face. "You have an unbelievable opportunity."

She shook her head. "I can't go back without you."

"I'm right here." He looked at her levelly in the eyes. "I'm right here, and I'll be with you the whole time."

She leaned back into the cushions.

"Think of everything you've discovered here. Think about all that you've learned about yourself. Think of all the things you can become."

She didn't want to *become* anything. She just wanted to be. And if she'd learned anything, it was that she did not have what it took to just *be* in a life filled with useless details and the ever-thinking brain—worries and squabbles and lightning-fast flashes of fear and dread, replaced just as quickly by joy or anger or sadness or elation.

She had tasted something of peace. And as hard as she'd fought to get home in the beginning, home was looking much more like a cabin in the woods to her now.

"This is not for you, not yet," he said. "You're not done."

She wanted to argue, but she thought that she'd always known it was true. It's why she didn't know her purpose here. It's why she questioned Lucy's stillness and Jon's quietude. It's why Sophie had unsettled her and why Anna eluded her. It's why Logi made her uncomfortable.

And then there was her mother and her father. And surprisingly, she found that she did have questions, even after living in this mystery with its strange twists and odd turns.

"I have to say goodbye to Lucy."

"Goodbye for now," he corrected.

"Do I have to say goodbye to now for you?"

He didn't answer, just pulled her up and guided her

out the front door. The moon was high in the velvet black sky, speckled with diamonds that were stars. The wind rustled the leaves, and the rapids murmured in the distance.

"All of this," he said, gesturing around him, "will be me talking to you. When you hear the water, I am laughing. When you hear the wind, I am singing. When you see the stars, I am smiling. Always, for you."

She nodded.

He kissed her tenderly on the lips. Then he smiled and walked down those rickety steps in the direction from whence they'd come earlier. She watched him until he was just a shadow, a trick of the moonlight. The opposite of the way he'd come. She'd wondered if he'd ever been here at all.

The wind kicked up, carrying with it the sound of the rapids closer to her ear. The stars glimmered through the leaves on the trees. And she knew that he was here. Always. For her.

☦ ☦ ☦

Lucy was waiting for her when she awoke the next morning. She wasn't watching Grace particularly closely, and she hadn't said anything out of the ordinary. But the energy was different today, and Grace knew that nothing would ever be the same again. Here. Or there.

Henry came in from the back door, wearing the same pair of baggy trousers that he'd had on the last time she'd seen him. He was also wearing a straw hat and a checked flannel shirt. She thought maybe it was too warm for his clothing, but he didn't look the least bit uncomfortable.

She was still wearing the unfamiliar shirts and shorts that had been Lucy's or her mother's.

Henry approached her. "Understand you're headed back," he said.

She didn't answer.

"I'm glad you'll give it another go. Lots of things to learn over there."

"Do I have a choice?"

"I expect we all have a choice about pretty much everything," he said.

Her body was sore, and her head throbbed with a dull ache. Then there was the painful lump in her throat that had been lodged there since she'd seen Brandon.

"Well, in any case," he said, "I'm glad I got to spend some time with you."

She looked at this man who was her grandfather, and she nodded, the lump growing. There was something unfair about all these goodbyes to these people who she shouldn't have known at all.

He looked like he knew she was going to cry and didn't want to, and he said, "Now, don't go getting all sappy on me."

That seemed to help, and she nodded.

"I *would* like you to do something for me if you get the chance."

"What?" she managed.

"Tell your mom that there was nothing to forgive in the first place. Can you do that?"

She nodded again, having no idea if she'd remember what he said. Or if she'd remember him at all. She half expected this whole place to fade like a dream. Because who was to say it wasn't?

Henry gave her shoulder another quick squeeze, and then he went back out the back door.

"He never was one for goodbyes," said Lucy quietly.

Grace stared at her, too—this woman who was so like her mother and yet, not.

"It's all going to be fine," she said, but Grace wasn't sure about that at all.

Lucy smiled with her serenity, and Grace just felt tired. Logi appeared from nowhere and wound around her legs, mewling like he knew something was going on. And maybe it was for him, too, because Grace didn't know if Lucy would stay there any longer without Grace there as her reason.

"Where will you go?" asked Grace.

Lucy tilted her head back. "There's no secret place that you go, exactly," she answered. "You simply… are.

You're everything and nothing all at once. The earth, the air, the sun, the water—your essence is in all of those things."

"But right now, you're in a cabin in the forest."

"Concentrated energy, as you are. Perceived by you, experienced by you."

Grace didn't answer.

"I am in a human form, but I will disperse and become a part of eternity. And I will become a part of you."

"And I will stay in human form."

"For now. You will grow and create and learn and love. And you'll remember."

"And Brandon?" she asked.

Lucy touched her heart. "He will live on in here." She tapped her head. "And here." Lucy continued. "Just like any other experience, you'll need to look back on it to understand it. Maybe that will be a day from now; maybe it will be a year from now. Or ten years from now. And maybe you won't understand it until it's all over. And that's okay too."

Grace could hear the clucking of the chickens outside, and when she looked out the window, she saw Jon bending over the coop and the girls chasing the chickens running freely around the back yard. She smiled. "There's a lot of life here."

"There is a lot of life everywhere. And beauty. You just have to look for it."

Grace was weary. Bone tired. It was still early in the day, but she thought she could sleep forever.

Anna and Sophie looked up at her in the window and waved. Grace waved back, and Jon smiled.

"Come," Lucy said. "Let's go to the river."

The river was running fast and free, the shallows cresting and swirling, the light sparkling and the shadows deepening. Beyond the rapids, the water seemed to slow and calm, but Grace knew that it was just as swift. The depth, though, gave it the perception of stillness. But it had a destination.

The air hung heavy around them, and Grace had the overpowering urge to step into that water and allow it to bathe her, to cool her, to carry her away. And she would let it. She would let it take her where it would. She would become the water—free, yet contained, swift in places and deep in others, but always bending and shaping around obstacles that didn't exist for it at all.

She looked at Lucy, whose whole being glittered in the morning sunlight beside her. She was so bright that she hurt Grace's eyes. Then she pixelated into a thousand diamonds. Grace knew it was a trick of the light, and she watched as Lucy reformed and smiled.

Grace smiled back, and then she did step into the water. It was brisk on her ankles and then her calves as she stepped into the rapids. Up to her knees, the water rushed against her legs, and she struggled slightly to stand upright against the strong rushing water.

And then she let go. There was an immediate shock and then a sigh.

She was aware of the rocks as she flowed, but as she became one with the river, she simply was. The sky was above her, and Lucy beamed down on her. She was consecrated and anointed. She was Grace.

# CHAPTER FIFTEEN

G race blinked awake. The light was artificial and bright. Blinding. It made her head hurt, and she shut her eyes again. This was not the clear light above the river.

She couldn't quite move, and she found that she was strapped down or restrained in some way. Blinking again, she squinted and saw a tube connected to her arm attached to a bag of some sort of liquid. As her awareness increased, she noticed a slow and steady beeping noise that kept time in the otherwise eerie silence.

Grace tried to talk, but her throat felt closed, and she gagged when she realized that there was something in her mouth. Her body thrashed with the effort to reach her mouth, and she tried again to yell. It came out as a moan or a gurgle.

A form in a vinyl chair next to the bed stirred, slowly at first, then coming to, more frantically. "Grace?" it asked, whispering. Then louder, "Grace, are you there?"

Her mother came into view, looking very much un-

Mariah-like. No makeup, short auburn hair sticking straight up in the back and flipped up in an unflattering way on the other side. Grace noticed all these things as, with her eyes, she begged her mother to help her.

Mariah held a steady hand against hers to stop her movement. She pressed a button, and a woman in a rumpled white outfit appeared. A nurse, Grace thought. She was in a hospital. The woman looked as though she had been there for quite some time. She came over quickly, and then another nurse, younger and fresher in a crisp frock, also joined them.

"Welcome back," the fresh one said, and the rumpled one said, "Just relax." She held a firm hand on Grace's shoulder.

Grace implored her with wide eyes as she struggled to stay calm. Mariah smoothed her cheek, and then, out of nowhere, her father was in the room, followed by a middle-aged male in a white lab coat. The man looked at her chart and examined her. Then he asked Grace if she thought she could breathe on her own.

Grace nodded vigorously because all she wanted was to get the thing out of her throat.

The doctor and two nurses came over and took off the tape holding the tube to her skin, then one of the nurses suctioned out her mouth. The doctor asked if she could cough, and she cough/gagged while the nurse gently pulled on the tube. The other nurse suctioned as she gagged, and the tube slid out of her throat. They made her cough a few more times and then spit into a small tray that one of the nurses held to the side.

"Your throat is going to be sore for a while," the doctor said. "But Lily and Rose will take good care of you. I'll be in to check on you in a little while." To one of the nurses, he said, "You can unstrap her arms." And to her parents, "Not too much time with her. She'll need plenty of rest. She'll be thirsty, but we'll want to keep an eye on that throat before she takes anything by mouth." He looked at Grace, arching a brow. "You're a lucky young lady."

She glanced over at her mother, who had her gaze trained on Grace, not the middle-aged doctor.

Her throat *was* sore, and she had trouble swallowing, but she did want a drink. When she asked for it, her father pointed to the IV in her arm. "This will keep you strong," he said.

Both he and her mother were standing remarkably close to each other, their arms touching, at her bedside. "I know you're tired, even though you just woke up," her mother said. "Do you remember what happened?"

Her father said, "Oh, Mariah, maybe not yet."

But Grace thought back, remembering Lucy first, and she said, "Lucy was there."

Mariah opened her mouth then shut it again. "No, not Lucy," she said quietly.

Grace saw her father put his hand on her mother's

back.

"The accident. Do you remember what happened before the accident?"

Grace shut her eyes then opened them again. "Brandon," she managed.

Her mother's mouth turned down at the corners, and she nodded.

"We should let her rest," her father said, and her mother listened to him. There was no nasty exchange or argument. There was also no hatred.

Grace reached out and touched her mother's arm. She coughed, swallowed painfully, then said, "Henry," she started, coughed again. She willed herself to speak. "You don't have anything to be sorry about."

Her mother's face brightened for a second and then seemed to freeze like that, suspended in time. And then it crumbled. Mariah covered her face with her hands, and her father guided her away. Over his shoulder, he said, "Gracie, we'll be right outside, okay? You rest."

Grace lay there, staring at the white ceiling tiles. There was a small brownish spot in the corner of one of the tiles, and she couldn't stop staring at it. She shut one eye. It was the silhouette of an old man.

She thought about Henry. There was no doubt that her experience had not been a dream, but she wasn't sure exactly what it had been.

She drifted off, then was awoken by the doctor, who had a different nurse in tow.

"How are you feeling?" he asked.

She managed a weak, "Okay, I think." Followed by, "How long?"

He scribbled something on the chart that he was carrying. "How long will you be here?" He didn't look up at her. "I'd like to keep an eye on you for a few more days. You have a nasty bump on your head, and you've been under for a while. Can't be too careful with a head injury. Your body's been through some trauma."

She reached up and felt the bandages there. Her chest also felt sore.

"How long since the accident?" she asked.

He looked up at her then, the first time that he looked like he really saw her. "Three days," he said. He snapped the file closed and looked at her. "You're probably going to have some lapses in your memory of that night," he said. "Some of that might be physical, but much of that will be your mind protecting you." He paused. "You know you lost a friend?"

She nodded. She preferred to think about Brandon in the forest and the cabin, kissing her softly before he disappeared into eternity. She remembered everything about that.

"Your blood-alcohol level was within normal limits," he continued. "But the police will want to talk to you about that night, too. You think you're up to that?"

She shut her eyes, and a tear leaked out. She didn't think she was ready for that.

"We don't have to do it now," he said.

"What do they want to know?"

He sat down on a stool next to the bed. "They'll want to ask you some questions about what happened at the party. We know where you were that night. Brandon had been drinking. We also did a full examination of you based on some information the police collected from some witnesses. A social worker will be in to talk to you about that, too. There's some trauma beyond...the trauma from the accident," he said gently.

She didn't answer.

"I have a daughter your age," he continued. "We do our best to keep our kids safe, but we can't be there all the time." He patted her hand. "This will all be okay for you. But for a while, it'll be harder than it should have been."

Grace thought about Lucy. Don't we always make it harder than it should have been? Was that part of the lesson that she needed to learn?

The doctor smiled at her kindly. "We'll be poking and prodding you for a few more days, but you're on your way," he said. "We'll have you back home before you know it."

The problem was, she didn't know where home was anymore.

☨ ☨ ☨

Her parents were in and out. It made Lucy uncomfortable every time they were together, hovering close to each other and Lucy. They whispered to each other when they thought she was sleeping and even when they knew that she was awake. It was as if this tragedy had smashed a wall and built a bridge that hadn't existed before. Maybe she would be thankful for it someday, but right now, it was just unsettling.

Nurses came in, and she gradually started sipping liquids. The catheter came out, and she could go to the bathroom. The IV stayed in for another day, and then it came out too, and she could eat solid foods, even though she didn't have an appetite. The bandage stayed on her head, and, with her eyes, she followed lights and fingers coming close to her nose.

Then the white bandages came off, replaced by a smaller flesh-colored patch.

She studied herself in the mirror in the bathroom, the ugly jagged stitched-up cut on her forehead poking out from behind the patch, the piece of hair shaved back from the place where the wound started near her hairline.

When she wasn't being poked and prodded, she slept. She dreamed of Brandon and Lucy, Henry and Jon. But she wasn't with them anymore. They were simply figments of her mind, perceptions of collected thoughts and memories.

A social worker named Nina came in and asked her

if they could have a conversation about what had happened at the party. Grace asked that her parents not be present for that discussion. She could tell that her mother was upset, but Mariah didn't push the issue.

Nina was kind, and Grace was honest. She told her about the events leading up to the bedroom scene and what had happened after. She tried to be fair, but given what had happened to Brandon, she knew that she would not be able to protect Tanner. Not that he deserved her protection. But they had all been through a lot.

She just wanted to tell the truth.

The police asked her questions, too, and asked if she'd like to press charges against Tanner. She said that she wanted to think about that. But she knew that her story would not be defined by what happened that night, regardless of her decision.

And then she was released, wheeled to the massive sliding doors at the exit of the hospital. Her mother walked with her, and her father pulled his car—a sturdy and practical SUV—to the front of the building.

"Where's your BMW?" Grace asked her mother.

"It's at home. We thought it would be best to drive together."

Her legs still wobbly, they helped her into the front seat, and her mother climbed in the back. With traffic, it took them about fifteen minutes to get out of the city. Grace watched the traffic as they drove, trying to recall anything at all from what had happened. But that memory was gone. The doctor told her that she might never remember, or one day it all might come rushing back in shocking clarity. She wasn't sure which she would prefer.

She could feel her father looking at her periodically from the driver's seat.

Her mother was quiet in the back.

When they were home, her mother walked next to her to the front door, and her dad walked behind them. Once inside, Grace looked around the townhouse, which was familiar but seemed far away. How strange that the cabin in the forest seemed much more real.

It even smelled unfamiliar, she thought, as they settled her on the sofa.

They stared at her expectantly.

She stared back.

"Are you hungry?" her mother asked.

"Not really."

"The doctor said you had to eat, even if you didn't have much of an appetite."

"I'll make you some soup," her father said brightly, leaving them alone.

Grace was uncomfortable with this deflated Mariah, who was someone, but not her mother.

"How long is he staying?" Grace asked. She wasn't trying to be unkind, but this amount of attention was unsustainable.

"As long as he wants."

Grace side-eyed her. "What about Shannon and the twins?"

"Well, of course, they understand."

But Grace detected a hesitation there, and she wondered what exactly it was that Shannon and the kids understood. She should have felt triumphant about finally having her father's attention, but she realized that it was never what she'd wanted.

What was it that she *had* wanted?

Her mother perched on the edge of the chair next to the sofa, a bird ready to take flight. "Some of your friends have asked if they could visit."

She tried to raise her eyebrows. But that hurt her head, and she looked levelly at her mother instead.

"Oh, not *those* friends," Mariah said, referring to the kids from the party. The ones with good parents and proper upbringing. "From the swim team," she corrected. "Ava, Kate, and Megan."

Grace was surprised. But then, not.

"I told them that you weren't up to it yet," her mother continued. "But maybe in a few weeks."

Grace tested out how she felt about that. It would be good to see them, but she was embarrassed by how she'd left them and how she'd gotten here. She was also embarrassed that they would want to visit her in the first place. She didn't think she would have been as gracious.

To her mother, she nodded. She would think about it.

"Has anyone else—" She didn't finish the question.

"No, but there is a police investigation into the party and what happened that night. Everything that happened at the Sherbondy house. I'm sure all the kids who had attended are all laying low right now." Mariah went quiet, then she wet her lips, and Grace knew what she was going to ask. "Have you considered pressing charges?" her mother said gently.

Grace leaned her head back against the cushions. Her dad appeared with the soup, saving her from the necessity of an answer at that moment.

She slurped some chicken noodle soup into her mouth while her parents watched her anxiously. She felt like she was seven again. No, probably even younger than that. Had she been seven, someone would have reminded her not to spill any soup on the furniture. There was no censure today.

She didn't finish the food but ate enough that she thought they would be satisfied. Her father leaned forward and took the bowl. "Are you tired?" he asked.

She *was* tired, but she didn't want to go to her bedroom just yet. "Can I just lie here for now?" she asked.

"Of course." Mariah scurried away to find a blanket and pillow and came back with them. When Grace was repositioned, she looked up at them as they looked down at her. And she smiled.

☦ ☦ ☦

When Grace woke again, her father was sitting beside her, reading. She stared at him for a moment. His pale face was more lined than she'd remembered. His eyes sunken behind his glasses, the lines fanning out deep into his cheeks. His sandy brown hair seemed thinner, but maybe she just hadn't paid any attention to him for a while. He did have a pleasant face. Calm. Not completely unlike the face of Jon, she thought with a touch of surprise.

He sensed her gaze and looked over. His mouth spread into a wide smile. "There you are," he said as if she'd been somewhere else for a time. "Feeling okay?"

She blinked and tested her head. "I'm okay," she affirmed. "Where's mom?"

"She ran to the office to pick up a few things. She thought maybe she could make it back before you woke up." He put his book down beside him and looked at her. "We're not going to leave you alone for a while."

Grace thought maybe that was more for them than for her. She propped herself up on an elbow and waved her father away when he tried to help.

He said, "I've been meaning to tell you about your phone."

Her phone, she thought. It had seemed like ages since she'd had one. She'd forgotten all about it.

"I bought you one, but I want to wait a few days to give it to you, just until you get settled. No need to worry yourself with the happenings of the world just yet."

He seemed nervous, and she could tell that he'd had this speech worked out ahead of time. The truth was, she had no interest in the phone. She knew there would have been news articles, especially considering who Nate and Tanner's parents were. And she certainly didn't want to read about the accident. She wanted to talk to people even less than that. She just said, "Okay," and that was that.

Her mother came rushing in the door then, her arms full of files. She took one look at Grace, and her face fell flat. "You're up," she said.

"She *just* woke up," her father reassured her. "I was explaining about the phone."

Her mother dumped the files on the decorative table next to the front door and came over to perch beside her. "We just think it would be better for you to wait to have a phone until you're feeling more yourself," she said.

Grace didn't know when that would be, but she said, "Mom, it's fine," maybe more harshly than she'd expected to.

Chastened, her mother pressed her lips together.

Grace lay back down and stared at the ceiling. She didn't want to have to tiptoe around her parents. This seemed reversed to her. She wanted to ask when her father was leaving, but she didn't dare do that now. She might crush him.

"Are you up to talking about something else?" he said, and Grace shut her eyes.

"Maybe now isn't a good time," her mother said, and something in her tone made Grace's blood feel icy in her veins.

"I have to go home tomorrow," he said. "It's been almost a week."

"You could always come back," Mariah whispered. Grace wanted to say, "I'm *right here*. I can hear everything you're saying." But she didn't. Instead, she asked, "What?" expecting an answer before they could talk themselves out of it.

They both hesitated as if they had forgotten she was there.

Mariah started, "Well, we've been thinking," she said, kneading her thin hands together in front of her. "The conversation that you and your dad had had before—" She stopped suddenly.

"Before the accident," her father finished. "About you coming to stay with us for your senior year."

Grace stared at them both. "What about it?" she asked slowly.

They both looked at her expectantly, but she refused to say anything until they spelled it out for her.

Mariah finally said, "We think it might be a good idea to think about staying with your father for a while. Not right now," she added. "Not until you'd feel up to it."

"But…why?" Grace asked, more stunned than anything else.

"Well," her father said awkwardly. "The high school in town is small, and you'll make some new friends. You'll get to know the twins a little bit better and the new baby."

Grace didn't want to do any of those things.

But the thing was, she didn't want to go back to her school either. She didn't want to be the subject of stares and whispers. She didn't want to be known as the girl who was assaulted and almost died. She didn't want to be known as Brandon McKay's girlfriend. The dead boy's girlfriend.

And the thing was, she wasn't even sad about him right now. She'd just seen him. But she knew she would be. And she wasn't sure she wanted all those people and the school itself to be a constant reminder of him.

"It's just an idea," Mariah said briskly, efficiently, and more Mariah-like than she'd been since before the accident. "We don't have to decide anything right now."

Her father started to say something else, and Mariah said, "Scott," in a warning tone.

He nodded. "I'm going to go call Shannon and the kids before bed."

Grace noticed that it was dark outside.

Mariah said, "You don't have to do anything you don't want to do. We just thought it might be a healthy change for you."

"What about you?" Grace asked.

"Oh, I'll be fine," she said airily. She laughed, but there was no joy in it. Then she seemed to give up the pretense and said, "I'll come to see you a lot. I don't mind the drive. Your dad always had family commitments. It was difficult for him to get himself up here." She hadn't said it unkindly, but she corrected herself quickly, "Not that he didn't think of you as his family. I just mean…you know." She faltered, and then her voice was strong again. "You and I—we were fine on our own for all those years. I'd always been very clear about that. About the fact that he didn't need to come." She sniffed. "I'm sorry about that." Her voice was softer with the last statement.

Grace looked closely at this woman, her mother. The tough veneer, the sharp edges. It had worn off for a time, but Grace didn't think it would be long before she'd build herself back up again. And before she did that, Grace needed to show her something.

"When can we take a drive?" Grace asked.

"A drive? Where?"

"To the house in the woods."

Mariah's mouth hung open for a second before she snapped it shut. "What house?"

"The house by the river. Where you grew up."

Mariah stood up and smoothed down her blue slacks with the palms of her hands. "I don't know why you'd want to go there."

"Because that's where Lucy is, and I think you need to make your peace."

# CHAPTER SIXTEEN

She'd missed Brandon's viewing and funeral service, but she had read the article about him in the Sunday edition of the printed newspaper that her mother still had delivered. It was a glowing article about his sports and academic accomplishments and what would have been his future plans for college and life. There was also ample mention of his father's standing in the community and his mother's charity work. There was no mention of the party that had led up to the accident. No mention of Grace. That story was playing out largely on social media.

She hadn't cried yet for him, but she did miss talking to him. Even though she knew he was with her, it just wasn't the same as having a conversation with a living, breathing person.

Her father went back to Shannon and the twins. He held her for a long time before he left and asked her to think about their conversation, but he did not push any further. He hugged her mom, too, which shouldn't have been a surprise after all they'd been through, but it still felt foreign to her. She couldn't get used to seeing them together, to seeing civility between them.

There was no more mention of her phone. Grace thought her mother must be waiting for Grace to ask her about it. But Grace wasn't in a rush for communication with the outside world just yet.

The day after her father left, while her mother was sitting at her home office desk, Grace stood in the door while Mariah leaned forward, squinting at something on the screen.

Grace waited until Mariah looked at her. "I'm feeling good, and it's a beautiful day outside. It might be a good day for a drive."

Her mother sighed and turned. "I don't think that's such a good idea."

"Why?"

There wasn't a good answer for that. But her mother said, "I know you dreamed of it, and you think you had an encounter with—" She hesitated, then finished, "those people—"

"Lucy, Henry, and Jon," Grace corrected.

Mariah turned the whole way around in her swivel office chair. She leaned forward. "Are you saying that you *met them*, or are you saying that they appeared to you, like floating in and out of a dreamscape?"

"I actually met them. I slept in a little bed with small pink flowers. I ate in the kitchen. I sat on the sofa with Lucy. I went fishing with Henry. I watched Jon whittle a limb to make a bow." She was ticking them off on her right hand, and Mariah held up her hand for Grace to stop.

"But that's impossible. That cabin has been vacant for nearly thirty years." Her mother leaned back in her chair and tilted her chin toward the ceiling. She said it more to herself than she did to Grace. "I'm not saying that I don't believe you. I do believe that you had some very vivid dreams." Her voice was uncertain.

Grace came into the room—a room she typically didn't enter—and sat down on the floor.

Her mother stood quickly. "Sit in my chair," she said, but Grace waved her away. "I'm fine."

She sat back down. "You see how it's impossible, though," she reasoned.

"I see how it would sound crazy, yes. But how else would I know?"

"Know what?"

The details came spilling out. "About your relationship with Jon. About how you came home early that fall and found Jon and Lucy in the kitchen. About what you said. About the fire—"

Mariah stood again. "Stop," she said firmly. She was breathing heavily. "I can't—You can't *know* any of that."

Grace was quiet. Maybe she had gone too far.

Mariah's phone buzzed on her desk, and she glanced at it. Then she snatched it up and typed in a reply. She dropped it heavily back down. "Okay," she said, her voice tired. "You win. We'll go."

Grace didn't want it to be about winning. She thought as she changed her clothes. She put on a t-shirt dress because it was easy and comfortable, but she winced as she worked it over her head. She still had bruises over most of her body.

Her mother was still sitting in her office when she came out of her room. Her phone buzzed as she held it in her hand. Grace stood in the doorway again. "Everything okay?"

She lifted a shoulder. "Sure." Her mother typed out another reply.

Grace didn't believe her, but she went downstairs to wait.

When Mariah appeared, her face looked drawn. "Okay, let's go." She strode briskly to the door, Grace following more slowly.

When she stepped outside in the late May sunshine, she realized this was the first she'd been outside since she'd come home from the hospital. The day was warm but not humid. It was one of those cloudless days with a light breeze and azure skies. A day that you just wanted to savor.

Her mother didn't seem to notice.

They climbed into her BMW and backed out of the driveway.

"Where is my car?" Grace asked as they pulled out onto the main road from their complex.

"It's gone," said her mother. "We'll think about a new one in a while."

Not that Grace had any interest in driving anywhere.

They rode in silence, but her mother's phone kept vibrating in the console between them. "Is that work?" Grace asked.

"It's Peter," Mariah answered.

"Why don't you call him?"

"I don't have anything to say."

Grace didn't ask any more after that.

After a few minutes, they entered the highway, headed south. She noticed her mother's hands gripped the steering wheel tightly.

Grace didn't feel especially worried about the journey or concerned that a crash was imminent. She was more nervous about being in the woods again, for some reason. She knew that no one would be there.

She leaned her head back and stared up at the sky through the sunroof. She wondered if Brandon was somewhere, thinking of her.

Her thoughts turned quickly to that night. She shifted in her seat. The anger and the shame welled up within her. She didn't think she could face her classmates, her teachers, even if she had the summer to put some space between what had happened and her return.

"Okay?" her mother asked, glancing toward her.

She nodded. "I've been thinking about what you and dad brought up. About staying with him for a while."

Mariah nodded slowly.

"I don't think it's a terrible idea to maybe start over somewhere new."

Mariah smiled, but Grace thought she seemed sad. "I don't think it is either." She reached over and squeezed Grace's hand.

Her phone buzzed again. "For god's sake," she exclaimed.

"What does he want?"

Her mother waved a hand. "I told him I needed to take some time, and he's not happy about it."

"About you spending time with me."

She didn't deny this. "To be fair, you were a teenager when we started to date and didn't need a lot of handholding. His children have been out of the house for years. He's forgotten what it's like."

Grace didn't think her mother should be making excuses for him, but she didn't say anything.

They merged from one highway onto another, this time heading east. "How far is it?" Grace asked.

"Oh, about an hour from here."

Grace settled in and watched the scenery pass. From the upscale neighborhoods that they'd just left to more rural farmlands that dotted the highway.

They finally turned off onto a less-traveled highway

and passed some dingy looking gas stations, run-down shopping complexes, and auto-repair businesses. The houses weren't large, and they weren't particularly well-kept. Lawns were too tall, and weeds were rampant. Everything looked tired and shabby.

After a few miles, they turned again, this time down a narrow road where weeds grew almost tall enough to reach into the road, if you could call it that. It may have been paved, but it was pitted with potholes and covered with gravel. Grace felt a niggling at the back of her mind. Some part of her remembered this.

She pushed the button for the window release, and when the window was down, she breathed in the scent of grass as they drove down the slight grade. Soon the vegetation thickened, and trees appeared. They turned once more into those trees. She could see that there had been a road of sorts here at one time. There was still some gravel over which they were driving.

She knew this place. "Have you been here recently?" she asked her mother.

Mariah shook her head, concentrating on the path in front of her. "I've been thinking about it a lot, though."

"Because of me?"

"After your accident—that night. We weren't sure how severe your head injury was. The doctors put you into a coma so that they could try to reduce the swelling. It felt like what had happened with Lucy, except she didn't wake up..." She inhaled and exhaled. "I dreamed of this place too, when I'd finally dozed off in the hospital waiting room."

"You dreamed you came here?"

"I dreamed I had driven down this road, just like we're doing now." She shook her head. "It feels surreal."

After what seemed like miles—Grace knew it wasn't because they were driving slowly—Mariah said, "I think this is it."

They turned right onto what was another nearly hidden path, and at the end was a small wooden cabin that was in complete disrepair.

Mariah stopped the car and stared up at it. She shook her head. "So strange," she said. "The last time I was here was when your grandfather was—" She stopped. "I'd come to say goodbye."

"How old was I?" Grace was thinking of the fishing.

"You weren't born yet."

Grace didn't argue, and they exited the car, shutting the doors lightly behind them in the silence of the woods. Grace could hear the familiar rush of the river. The intermittent call of birds to each other through the tops of the trees. The sun-dappled the space around them. Grace smiled.

They walked up to the house, picking their way up the rotting boards of the porch. One side of the porch had completely fallen in, giving the place a lopsided appearance. A rocking chair, the wicker seat falling through, sat alone in the corner. Grace tried to see or sense Lucy here, but there was nothing.

Mariah pushed the door to the cabin open, and the smell of damp, stale mildew hit Grace first. This was not the place where she'd lived.

The setup of the house was the same. Beer bottles and trash were strewn around the interior. Either some homeless person had been squatting here, or kids used it as a place to party.

The stairs that led to the second floor had collapsed in on themselves, and Grace glanced up at the ceiling above her.

"Your grandfather built this place," her mother said. "He'd be sad to see this."

But Grace knew that this house didn't look this way in Henry's existence.

The bookshelves held a few old and faded books that were damp and filled with mold. Grace went over to them but didn't touch them.

The kitchen still had patches of the linoleum floor in place, but weeds had started growing up through holes in the floorboard beneath. Other than the old sink and counter, the room was empty.

"When was the last time grandma was here?"

"She left after your grandfather passed. Not too long after Lucy died. She got a good settlement from the railroad, headed to Florida, and never looked back."

Grace heard a voice, a whisper, toward the front of the house. Then she heard a scampering sound. She turned around, but her mother was still standing in that kitchen facing the back wall of the house. A shaft of light had appeared suddenly in some break in the ceiling. Grace turned around walked carefully toward the living area. She walked out the front door.

She heard her mother say, "Oh, Lucy." Another voice, carried on the wind, whispered, "Mariah."

Grace went to the river then and watched the sun dancing off the rapids, like glitter. She shut her eyes, breathed in the scent of the water, felt the warmth on her face. She wasn't sure how long she stayed like that. When she turned around, she saw the fading figures of a man and two small children. It could have been a trick of the light, but she knew that it wasn't.

But she blinked at they were gone. In the spot where they had been standing, she saw something moving around in the vegetation. As she approached, a small white kitten leapt into her view.

"Brandon," she exclaimed and picked it up, nuzzling it against her face.

The kitten purred and curled itself into her neck.

After some time, her mother emerged from the house. Her eyes were red, her lips white, her posture slightly stooped.

Grace came up to her. "Are you okay?" she asked.

Mariah stared at her. "I had no idea," she answered.

The breeze picked up and rustled the tops of the trees. The sudden shift seemed to break Mariah's reverie, and she smiled and straightened. "We should go," she said. Then she noticed the kitten. "What's this?" She lifted a knuckle, and the kitten nuzzled it.

"This is Brandon."

Her mother looked like she was going to say something and then thought better of it. "Good to meet you, Brandon," she said, bending her head close and stroking a finger between the kitten's green eyes.

"We can keep him?" Grace asked.

"Of course we can," Mariah answered.

They walked toward the car together.

As they backed down the driveway, Grace stared up at the house and saw Lucy watching from the window. She raised her hand, and her aunt smiled and waved back. Then she disappeared, finally at peace.

As they drove out of the woods, Grace felt a profound sadness. She knew she'd never come back here. But she was also infinitely appreciative of what she'd been given. A second chance. A new opportunity to learn. Another moment to live.

Brandon mewed in her lap, and she looked into his wide green eyes.

Her mother drove carefully out of the forest, and Grace caught a glimpse of the river running fast between the trees.

"As long as I live, I'll never forget this place," Mariah said. "It's in my bones, I think."

Grace looked at her. She saw Lucy in her mother's face, too. "Thanks for coming here."

"Thanks for coming home to me."

Grace leaned her head on her mother's shoulder for a second.

They too were at peace.

☦ ☦ ☦

www.ingramcontent.com/pod-product-compliance
Lightning Source LLC
Chambersburg PA
CBHW050254110726
47898CB00007B/2405